M000307683

THE GEORGE STORIES

THE GEORGE STORIES

by CHRISTOPHER GOULD

atmosphere press

Copyright © 2019 by Christopher Gould

Published by Atmosphere Press

Cover design by Nick Courtright
nickcourtright.com

No part of this book may be reproduced
except in brief quotations and in reviews
without permission from the author.

This book is a work of fiction. Names,
characters, places, and incidents are products
of the author's imagination or are used fictitiously.
Any resemblance to actual events or locales
or persons living or dead is entirely coincidental.

The chapter "Fall Mixer"
originally appeared in *The Binnacle*.

The George Stories
2019, Christopher Gould

atmospherepress.com

*I would like, with all due affection,
to dedicate this book to my family*

PROLOGUE

The Martians.

They were very East coast: L.L. Bean, Wegmans, apple picking, cross-country skiing and that sort of thing. Though not quite New Englanders, they were domiciled to that heart-grey, snowmelt portion of upstate New York that if judged by pictures alone might well have been mistaken for a landlocked version of Cheever's fair St. Botolph's or some other Northeasterly, jerkwater place.

Martin Martian, head of household, was a native of Saratoga, and spent the bulk of his youth in Spier Falls swimming holes and betting on ponies. His mother died during childbirth and his father during the Great War. He was thus, virtually from the outset, an orphan. Lineage-wise, Martin was predominantly of English-Scottish descent. As a boy, there'd been dinner-table claims that a distant relative had sailed over on the Mayflower. Another relative had gone so far as to claim that the man's spectacles were behind glass in a Philadelphia museum. Martin's most salient quality, besides his love for his family, was his all-around, plain-as-day niceness. He was impossibly tall; both long-legged and long-torsoed; his wiry frame a perfect complement to his wire-framed glasses. He'd begun his career as a P.E. teacher at Prosper High, before moving up the public school food chain to athletic director. It was here, at this post, that Martin fell victim to some "'bad math,'" and because of the subsequent budgetary fallout, was forced to leave the field altogether. No less than a week later, Martin opened an insurance business in town, a field where his stalwart affability and charm could pay dividends.

Joyce Ann Dobbs was a breathtakingly unsentimental girl who had been in the employment of the aforementioned school district as head nurse. It had been on February 6th, 1964, at the romantic hour of 6:24 a.m. that confirmed bachelor Martin, 36, had proposed to said chain-smoking nurse, all of 22, after no more than a third date. Joyce, being so swept off her high-arched feet, responded, "I guess so." That summer, they 'mooned in Quebec, and there on the fourth floor of the Chateau Frontenac, marriage was in due course consummated (though not without some coaxing on part of the dear groom, for the young bride, shall we say, was wholly unprepared for a certain uncircumcised male body part).

Joyce was the ideal sort of 1960's wife—the kind that could cook, clean, and give one a semi-passable time in the sack. Her only true vice was the occasional Pal-Mal—well that, and a rather harmless twice-a-week thrift-store addiction. While she was prone to histrionics (she, by her own admission, "came from a long line of worriers"), she was generally regarded as pioneer-era-tough, a byproduct perhaps of depression-era parents. Joyce was exactly 25% Italian on her mother's side and rest of her, well, was largely unaccounted for. She was Roman-nosed and dark-complexioned, lending her a fine pulchritude regardless of daylight hour or angle. Religiously speaking, she was raised Catholic, attended parochial school, not to mention the obligatory Sunday mass with her family. But the collective experience had, as a whole, done little for her spiritually and thus since the age of 18, she'd been essentially nonpracticing. Her only sibling was a brother, two years her senior—a self-described 'career homosexual' who constantly took hegiras between Albany and the Berkshires in a late-model Volvo.

The Martians inherited the house on 424 Weaver Street from Martin's side of the family—a grandmotherly old Tudor with a backyard that bordered a long-since-defunct apple orchard. The house itself was a five-bedroom job with a screened-in back porch. Due to proximity to the orchard, a series of non-sanctioned apple trees were scattershotted throughout the Martian's rear-most portion of the backyard (mostly Red Delicious and few Cortlands). As for Weaver Street itself, it was an old street with retired people—not a single young couple with exception to the Martians could have been identified on the census bureau register within a three-street radius. But as Martin Martian liked to say, "A mortgage-free house is, hell, a mortgage-free house."

In the couple's earliest, pre-kid years they could be seen driving 'round town in a 4WD green-tinged Grand American, complete with a non-functioning CB radio antenna suctioned to the passenger side of the hood. The Martians, virtually from the outset, were "joiners," as in they wished, rather resolutely, to not miss out on anything. In fact, during that first year on Weaver Street alone, they volunteered for the local historical society, the chamber of commerce, Boys and Girls club, and headed up a Fresh-Air kid program. In the next, Joyce signed on to Hospice and Meals on Wheels while Martian became a weekend driver for ambulatory veterans. While there was a certain degree of altruism at the heart of these undertakings, the Martians wanted, first and foremost, to be a part of things, to from a communal perspective, be perceived as respectable—and in that they did. In fact, during those pre-kid years of marriage, the sole organizations they declined to be a part of were the local chapters of the Democratic and Republican parties: the crux of the issue was that the Martians were apolitical, neither having ever registered, let alone voted, in a single presidential or, for the matter, gubernatorial election. Thus, their Laodicean nature, kept them focused strictly with the familial and communal.

The Darby and Joan Weaver Street dynamic was broken up in May of 1968, when Annabelle Christine Martian was born, and with that, all volunteer work on the part of the young couple ceased. Annabelle was all dark hair and eyes; a sort of Italian Shirley Temple. She was undeniably lovely, most especially about the face and eyes. Annabelle was christened at St. John's, the local Catholic Church, but despite assurances from the Martian's, their attendance at Mass remained spotty. As a first-born child, she was doted on and read to every night. Her days were occupied by playdates, dance lessons, and swim trips to the local Y. Things came easily for the girl: like her father, she was a first-rate swimmer and like her mother, she was a model student who seemingly, perhaps innately, knew the answers to every test. Along with this was the cardinal fact that Annabelle was a charmer, the sort of child who could uncannily command a room.

Family-tree-wise, we now come to the subject of George. He was born on the hottest of summer days: August 1, 1973, some two weeks overdue. Following a nine-hour, epidural-free labor, George emerged from the furnace between his mother's legs red and clammy—not unlike a just picked, but somehow overripe, tomato. He was an 11-pounder—a statistic that not only caused his mother immeasurable labor pain but also resulted in her harboring a vague, unspoken resentment toward him from that day the forward. It goes without saying that the Martians loved George upon arrival, but through no fault of their own fell into a spell of second-born child-complacency. He was quiet; an observer; a heavy sleeper whose docile and affable nature made him, at least in comparison to Annabelle, unremarkable. In truth, the only noteworthy things about the boy in those early years were his excessive bedwetting and a penchant for creating mind-bogglingly extravagant Lego and Erector Set showpieces. During daylight hours, he could usually be found on a backyard swing set or the adjacent sandbox, and, when confined to interiors, was prone to staring, open maw, at one of his sister's innumerable books.

It's worth noting that George and Annabelle, at least in those early years, got on swimmingly. While there were intermittent squabbles over who got the last cookie or what cartoon to watch, they were, by and large, the best of playmates. In warmer months, they were partial to hide-and-seek, tree climbing, and spirited rounds of Connect Four. In winter, snow forts and sledding occupied the bulk of their time. As a family, the Martians vacationed in Williamsburg, Virginia, Niagara Falls, and the Baseball Hall of Fame and, save for a thousand pettifogging details, the closest thing resembling a crisis was when George left his beloved "blanky" behind at an I-95 Will Roger's.

Thus, the long and short of it was that those early years were a triumphant, idyllic time for the Martians—the sort that one might reminisce about while thumbing through an old photo album. But then, one night, in the fall of '76', when Annabelle was quarantined by a siege of chicken pox,

George (all of 3) crawled out of his crib and, without warning, completed her fifth-grade mathematics homework (multiplication and long division). As he'd sat crossed-legged on the new shag carpet, he'd then moved on to diagramming sentences, determining lines of longitude and latitude, and finished off by compiling a five-page test that he ostensibly labeled, "Cumulative Final Exam." Upon discovery, the Martians were wide-eyed, and Annabelle, well, worry-logged. For up till that moment, she'd been the family star, a fata morgana of sorts. And so, as she stood bathrobed next to her parents, with her chicken-poxed body itching hellishly, she gave George a wraith-like glare and turned to her parents and smiled, claiming the whole thing had been a ruse, an elaborate pre-planned joke on her part: that in actuality she'd done the assignments. The Martians could only smile, pat Annabelle on the head, and laugh heartily as they returned to an episode of *60 Minutes*.

It would be several months later, semi-ironically, at Annabelle's glowing parent–teacher conference, when George's ascribed virtue as "boy genius" would formally come to light. He'd been left unattended on a school library floor while opposite him, over a shoulder-high bookcase, the aforementioned powwow was underway. Initially, the boy had been deposited in the children's section, but somehow—perhaps through innate magnetism—ended up in reference. Here, staring vacant-eyed in his usual bookish manner, George began mugging up the librarian's rather codified take on the Dewey decimal system by pulling book after book off the shelves:

Lend Me Your Ears: Great Speeches in History
Portable Speeches (the Complete Unabridged Edition)

World Anthology of Famous Orators
Great Words from Great Minds (Second Edition)
Wordmasters: A Rhetorical Analysis of Famous Speeches

With the volumes splayed at his feet, George picked one up, opened it, and proceeded to give it what might best be described as an ocular pawing—a surgical eye-scan. With his head bowed, he stared unblinkingly at the pages for no more than a few misbegotten seconds and then dropped the volume before moving on to the next. Ten minutes later, the boy began reciting Martin Luther King's "I Have a Dream" speech," verbatim. As his plangent, sing-song voice reverberated through the library, the Martians, Annabelle, and Mr. Pugh (Annabelle's teacher of record) rose to their feet. Rounding the bookcase, the rather outsized group caught sight of George reciting MLK word for word, without so much as glancing at the pages. After a few gasps and several are-you-seeing-what-I'm-seeing glances, George went on, uninterrupted, till he not only recited Mr. King in his entirety but also the unabridged versions of JFK's Inaugural Address and MacArthur's Farewell Address to Congress. When he at last finished, George looked up at the fifty-odd onlookers who had assembled and smiled, but gave no explanation.

At the urging of Mr. Pugh (himself a card-carrying member of Mensa), George was evaluated soon after in accordance with the newest, most scientific of methods: his IQ, a whopping 136. The test administrator, a Dr. Strauss, went on to say that the events in the library were "no parlor trick," but rather that George was born with a "first-rate eidetic brain;" he had a photographic memory.

It should be noted that time-wise, George's big reveal coincided with his father's rather abrupt dismissal as Athletic Director (a salary of $97,000). Adding to the ugliness, not to mention the chapfallen nature of the sacking, was the cardinal fact that the family had just the week prior signed off on a rather extravagant in-ground pool installation (the details of which involved a state-of-the-art heat pump and a custom-built pool house, patterned in a funky, Spanish mosaic). Thus, while the Martians were thrilled for George and his long-term promise, their financial health was foremost in their mind. For, in addition to the monthly bills that had to be paid, there were now (courtesy of the pool) several ungodly balloon payments on the horizon.

One evening, as Mr. and Mrs. Martian huddled for a rather emotional bill-slashing session, Mr. Pugh rang the bell. The YMCA membership had been deep-sixed. So, too, had the family's second car, not to mention cable. And so, as Mrs. Martian opened the door, she was bereft of her usual housewifely glow, and in its place was a waterfall of tears. After relaying the family plight with an air of Iran–Contra-like secrecy, Mr. Pugh could only smile. He then pulled a high-gloss brochure from the inner lining of his jacket and suggested that George try his hand at the "gravy train" that was the children's talent show circuit, and soon, plans were set in motion.

CHAPTER 1: THE CONTESTANT

There were twenty-four contestants in the snack line, and the way they were swarming about the cookie tray, Mrs. Martian had been unable to get her un-manicured hands on but a single chocolate chip or even a lousy molasses for her son George. And so, instead of fighting off waves of high-achievers and one particularly gluttonous southpaw, she had, for the last ten minutes, occupied herself by reading over the talent show program, applying fresh coats of Chapstick, and just now, was in the midst of mentally redecorating the Newhouse Theater's main lobby.

Demographically speaking, the crowd was almost strictly of the upward-mobility type—the sort that chiefly resided in suburban areas; attended quality schools; took vacations; and had good credit ratings, financial advisors, and college savings plans. All good things. Good qualities, American-dream-type stuff. But insofar as one contestant was concerned, the assemblage was an altogether caviling and nasty bunch, categorically defined by parents hell-bent on cattle-prodding their children to that ever-marketable and esteemed realm known as Success.

Presently, Mrs. Martian was running her hand compulsively through her bob of a hairdo as though she were in perpetual fear of being exposed as a victim of early-stage female-patterned hair loss. Every so often she'd break up her routine to bird-dog the marplotters at the cookie tray, but with no break in the line was condemned to the rather onerous task of waiting. One, two, and just now 3.125 seconds later, she raised her left hand to the window behind the bench she was sitting on and pressed her palm to the glass as if by some great miracle the November coldness would, by proxy, elicit a lenitive effect. With no luck, she dropped her hand to her lap and as she smoothed out the hem of her blue tartan dress, the 44-year-old mother of two felt a sudden tap on her shoulder:

"How's George?" Randall F. Dobbs asked.

Mrs. Martian stared at her brother for a moment, as though the very question were somehow unanswerable and then rose to her feet. Above her, a large, rather extravagant banner read, *Welcome to the National Junior Talent Show Final: $50,000 Grand Prize!*

"Don't ask, Randall. Don't ask," Mrs. Martian said as her voiced cracked an octave or two. "I've a *terrible* feeling he's headed for a *terrific* fall."

Randall F. Dobb's unibrow twitched just perceptibly as he digested this particular piece of information. "Don't be silly," he said after a moment, "George'll be just fine. Why, the last time I saw him-"

"Don't argue with me Randall," Mrs. Martian said as she raised her hand in protest. "You're just as bad as Marty. I mean, *I'm* his mother and *I* oughtta know: something's very, very wrong."

Dobbs made a little windshield-wiper motion of his head, "Where"s the kid now?"

"God only knows," Mrs. Martian said as she retook her seat on the uncushioned bench. "Told me he was going for a walk."

Dobbs ran the palm of his left hand through his greyed hair and sighed, "Marty here?"

"Annabelle's got a swim meet," Mrs. Martian said. "Ithaca."

Dobbs nodded and then sat down. There was about a four-inch buffer between them.

"What I don't get," Mrs. Martian said as her voice bordered on the hysterical, "what I can't possibly understand is why he's so damn unhappy. I mean, here he is, as talented as all hell, I mean a genius even, and he wants *nothing* to do with *any* of this," she said waving the talent show program.

Dobbs leaned in close and squinted his blue-hazel eyes, "So what happened *this* time? I mean, what set him off?"

"Oh, he's miffed about being the last contestant," Mrs. Martian said as she wiped off a piece of lint from her left shoulder. "Doesn't want to wait."

"Is that all?" Dobbs asked pointedly.

Mrs. Martian crossed her legs and swallowed, "Oh, I *may* have said something about him being the local dandy. You know, the showstopper, but I was *only* trying to cheer him up."

Dobb's grimaced. "Why would you go and say something like that? You know perfectly well-"

"Look, I was *only* trying to cheer him up," "Mrs. Martian said, expelling a breath. "Besides, if he can't accept a simple compliment from his *own* mother, then what's the point?"

Dobbs sat back on the bench, his posture suggesting he wasn't about to argue. "I just think you need to be more delicate with him is all. I mean, the two of you have been on the road every weekend for very nearly a year. That would take a toll on *any* 8-year-old, even a prodigy."

There was a faint glisten of perspiration on Mrs. Martian's forehead and as she turned to face her eldest brother, her confidant, she ran a finger over her brow. "Oh,

I'm well aware of the toll it's taking. I''ve got the hotel receipts to prove it. I'd just like a little appreciation from him. I mean, do you know what I caught him reading?"

Dobbs shook his head. In the distance, there was a crackle and hiss of a faulty overhead P.A. system.

"Here," Mrs. Martian said as she finger-pushed a rather thickset volume into her brother's lap.

Dobbs took hold of the book and, in a manner peculiar and probably limited to a person afflicted with astigmatism, squinted his eyes till they were very nearly closed:

Child-Stars: The Psychological Fallout of Gifted Children

"Where in God's name did he get this?" Dobbs asked after a moment.

Mrs. Martian frowned. "Sutherland."

"The professor?"

Mrs. Martian nodded. "I tell you, I never liked him from the start. I mean, from the first minute he started testing George, he's been filling his head with all sorts of wild ideas."

Sutherland was a Cornell man, a professor emeritus of Big Red's renowned Human Development department. He'd learned of George by way of a newspaper clipping posted, rather precariously, on a bulletin board in the far reaches of Martha Van Rensselaer Hall. He'd been working with George for the past six-odd months, coming away with the impression that the boy was but a few mind-bending sessions away from making several Einstein-like breakthroughs. Sutherland was prone to speaking with a well-practiced Ivy League inflection emanating chiefly, but not exclusively, from the bottom-third of his voice box. It was the kind of voice that tended to grate on his listener—most especially those who fell into the non-matriculating category.

"Have you spoken to Sutherland?" Dobbs asked as he adjusted his seated position.

Mrs. Martian shook her head. "And that's not the worst of it. Look what chapter he was reading."

Dobb's thumbed through the book till he found the page that was dog-eared. "Dealing with high-pressure parents," he read aloud.

"Keep going," Mrs. Martian instructed. "Read the part George underlined."

Dobbs' eyes scanned the page until they pinpointed the section that had been underlined. After pausing to clear his throat, he once again read aloud:

"Parental enthusiasm can oftentimes create an atmosphere of strain whereby the gifted child, regardless of achievement, can never quite fulfill the ever-increasing demands that are placed upon him."

"Keep going," Mrs. Martian said as she folded her arms in disgust.

Dobbs nodded obligingly and then continued:

"In such instances, the gifted child may develop anxiety issues, depression, insomnia, and, most regrettably, can fall victim to suicide."

"It's awful isn't' it? Just plain awful," Mrs. Martian said rhetorically. "I mean the very idea that Marty and I-"

Dobbs tossed the volume on the bench and sat back. "Has he been acting funny?" he interrupted. "I mean, peculiar?"

Mrs. Martian sat up a trifle straighter on the bench. Behind her, a mix of sleet and snow had begun to fall. "I wouldn't say peculiar. Just the *usual*: you know, the tantrums, locking himself in the bathroom, that funny business with the mirror, all that sort of stuff."

Dobb's expelled a sigh and nodded. To his right, a girl passed by on roller skates. "It hasn't got any worse though, has it?"

Mrs. Martian's face crimsoned up as though she was withholding information.

"Come on Joyce. Out with it," Dobbs demanded.

Mrs. Martian stared immutably into space for a few seconds and then turned back to face her brother, blinking her eyes not once:

"I found a picture in one of his notebooks," she said.

Dobbs leaned forward with renewed interest, "A picture? Of what exactly?"

Mrs. Martian felt at her throat critically and gulped. "He drew a picture of himself in a coffin. Flowers and everything,'" Mrs. Martian said tearfully.

"Jesus," Dobbs said, his eyes opening at full aperture. "Talk about morbid."

"That's an understatement," Mrs. Martian said, dabbing at her eyes.

"Well, we've got to do something," Dobbs said.

Mrs. Martian gave her brother a quick glance and then stared out the window. "I did," she said. "I spoke to your psychiatrist friend last night."

Dobbs leaned in close. "Gerard? Well, it's about time. What did he say?"

Mrs. Martian watched for a moment as a boy traipsed by holding his mother's hand. He was more or less George's age. "I had to tell him all the background information," she said glancing back to the window. "The locked doors. The tantrums. The funny business with the mirror. And the picture, of course."

"And?"

Mrs. Martian licked her lips and paused. Outside the window, everything was grey with snowmelt. "The first thing he said was that he needed to meet with George *in person*. He made that *very* clear. But that based on what I told him, he thought there was a chance he might try something."

Dobbs squinched up his face, the wrinkles in his forehead matching those of his khakis. "Whatddya mean, try something?"

"Well he didn't say exactly," Mrs. Martian said as she turned to face her brother. "He just said that in situations like these, things can escalate . . . you know, quickly . . . and that there was a slight chance, mind you *slight*, that he might. . ."

"Might what?" Dobbs asked impatiently.

"Well . . . hurt himself."

Dobbs abruptly stood up, "Hurt himself? Actually, hurt himself?"

"Calm down," Mrs. Martian said in a throaty whisper. She then looked quickly to her left and right, "Don't make a scene."

"I *will* make a scene," Dobbs said hostilely. "This is *George* were talking about. George! We have to take him home. Now! Get'em to Gerard."

Mrs. Martian gazed up at the banner on the wall, her eyes lingering on the part that read, "*$50,000 Grand Prize!*" and then looked back at her brother. "I am *not* going home," she said rather emphatically, "I just got here."

"Come on Joyce. Be sensible," Dobbs said.

Without warning, Mrs. Martian reached over and tugged at her brother's sleeve until he had again retaken his seat. "Look," she said, I didn't' drive eight hours for nothing. Besides, this is the finals, Randall. The finals! George has a *real* shot at winning this thing."

Dobb's gave his sister a hard stare, "You've got to pull him out."

There was a brief pause in the conversation as a boy carrying a magician hat in one hand and a small, semi-undernourished rabbit in the other paused mid-stride before them. When his parade of an entourage caught up, he walked on.

"What does Marty think?" Dobbs asked once the boy passed.

"Who? Mr. Pollyanna?" Mrs. Martian said incredulously. "He's useless in these situations. Useless!"

Dobb's issued his sister a conciliatory nod. "Still, I'd like to get *his* take. You know, just to get a little perspective."

"Go ahead. Give him a call," Mrs. Martian said indignantly. "Be my guest!"

Dobbs moved his right foot as he narrowly missed having a woman passing by from stepping on toes. He gave her a quick once-over and then turned back toward his sister.

"I don't know if I can be a part of this, Joyce," he said. "I just don't know."

"Look," Mrs. Martian said, "the doctor said there was only a *slight* chance he might try something. *Slight*," Mrs. Martian emphasized. "Besides," she added, "there are two of us here to keep an eye on him. *Two*. I mean, what could possibly go wrong?"

Dobbs looked at his sister and frowned. "It's a big risk."

"I know it is," Mrs. Martian said pursing her lips together. "But how can I back out now? I mean do you have any idea what $50,000 could do for him? For this family?" Mrs. Martian scratched the tip of her nose. "Not to mention *all* the other offers. The last kid who won ended up with own PBS special!"

Dobbs stared at his sister for several seconds, his Adam's apple of a neck a show all its own. "And I suppose there's no way of changing your mind?"

"How can I?" Mrs. Martian said throwing her hands up in the air. "I mean, do you *really* expect me to?'" she asked rhetorically. "Think about it for a second," Mrs. Martian went on. "Think about how much *we* struggled as kids. I mean, no college loans. Can you imagine that? No college loans!"

Mrs. Martian waited for a response, but when none came, she continued, "I mean my goodness Randall," she said with an air of overwrought emotion, "I had to work two jobs and you three! Don't you remember that? Don't you?"

Dobbs stared back at his sister and for a fractional moment he seemed unwilling or unable to speak. "Of course, I remember," he said after a moment. "Of course. I mean asbestos removal wasn't exactly glamourous. I mean, God only knows what I was exposed to."

Mrs. Martian leaned in close as though in an effort to sympathize. "And don't forget about the pest removal service. You used to come home smelling like dead mice and covered in bee stings for God's sake!"

Dobbs issued a few shakes of the head. He then waited for a hipless girl carrying a baton to pass by before he spoke. "What about you, Joyce? I mean, it can't be easy with

Marty getting sacked."

Mrs. Martian looked down at the carpet and then looked back up again. There was an abrupt watery-like quality to her eyes. "It isn't good. It isn't good at all."

"What about the insurance business?" Dobbs asked cheerfully. "That's gotta be up and running by now, right?"

Mrs. Martian reached into her pocketbook and pulled out a travel-sized package of tissues. "He's got one client so far, Randall. One! And even that's a little sketchy."

"You know," Dobbs said, "If you ever needed a little cash, I'd be more than willing-"

Mrs. Martian grimaced and shook her head. To her right and left there was an increase in traffic flow as though people were making a mad dash for their seats. "I'm not taking your money, Randall," she whispered. "And don't you dare mention it again!"

Dobbs tilted his head sideways and pulled at his ear, "Then what exactly do you want?"

"You know exactly what I want," Mrs. Martian said as she crumpled up a tissue. "Help me get George through this. I just can't pull him out of this thing now. I mean, we're just so damn close."

Dobbs expelled a breath, his face the very model of one who was deeply, perhaps even monumentally, conflicted. "Promise me you'll take him straight home after this," he said after a moment. "Promise me."

Mrs. Martian raised her right hand in an oath-like manner, "Honest to God, Randall. Honest to God," she said. "Just as soon as this thing is over."

Dobbs gazed up at the banner and then looked back at his sister. "Okay then," he said reluctantly, "I just hope you know what you're doing," and rose to his feet.

George Martian stood rear of stage of the Newhouse Theater leaning against a large, rather amateurish-looking mural of William Shakespeare that was painted on the far wall. He had a dominant-gene-oriented face: brown eyes, brown hair, detached earlobes, rollable tongue, and a sublime dimple on each cheek, which incidentally, were about the size of poker chips. He was not so much as handsome but, rather, wholesome looking, such that if he had the proper connections he might well be chosen for the cover of a Sears and Roebuck mail-order catalog (the kind the Martian family often had lying about their den coffee table, which, ostensibly, always seemed to be dog-eared and covered in leftover morning Fruit Loops).

As George squared his Buster Brown feet, he took a few steps forward and peaked through a mauve-colored side curtain where a boy on stage was in the midst of a semi-passable juggling routine. He was 10 or thereabouts, George guessed, and after a few moments of bird-dogging, he took a few small-boy breaths and ducked back behind the curtain.

It was all so pointless, George mused. Fraught with endless picture-taking and pageantry in order to fill the unfillable. For parental expectation was a near-depthless thing. At least that's what Sutherland said. After all, the crowd would be littered with parents hoping and praying that their child would outmeasure all others, leaving the rest, for all intents and purposes, to be spat upon. But this was not the time for kvetching, he thought; he needed to be in-the-now.

Just inside the curtain, on a small folding table, lay a stack of talent show programs, and, as George passed by, he two-fingered a copy between his hands and began thumbing through it. He then continued down a long, semi-lit passageway. From the opposite end, an enormous man decked out in a tuxedo and a rather severe comb-over was coming toward him carrying an archaic-looking microphone between his hands. As the man passed George, he put out his right hand and grazed the top of the boy's head, saying something to the effect of, "Break a leg, kiddo, break a leg!"

At the end of the passageway, George noted that his name had, for about the fifth or sixth time, been misspelled (Martin instead of Martian) and with a quick, near-violent movement, crumpled up the program and flung it into an overfilled garbage bin. He then sat down in the half-darkness on an errant folding chair and pulled out a small, journal-style notebook. As he began to read over his most recent entries it was as though he was suddenly transplanted into his very own private screening room:

September 7th
Annabelle is taking too deep a cut on her breaststroke. Must figure out a way to broach the subject—she's been especially touchy lately.
September 15th
Professor Sutherland is very kind to send all those books. Magnanimous even. I just wish he wouldn't be so hard on Mother.
September 21st
The concierge at the hotel would only let me take one cookie. When I asked for a second, he told me I was being kittenish. I don't think he knew what the word meant.
October 7th

I seem to have some degree of prenatal memory: more specifically, I recall being in Mother's womb. In the hopes of having an intelligent dinner conversation the other night, I tried mentioning this to the parentals, but they wanted no part of it. Sutherland is right: they're not deep thinkers.

October 9th

Random thought #102: I find it acceptable to dog-ear paperbacks, but not hardcovers. Not sure why.

Random thought #103: I can't understand why Uncle Randall has never married, but always has plenty of buddies around.

October 29th

Recently learned words: abortive, quid pro quo, puerile, insomniac, infanticide, alacrity, gimcrack, untenable.

Words to look up: polychromatic, hypermnesia, sui generis, deipnosophist, omphaloskepsis, ab ovo.

Abruptly, George reached into his suit-coat pocket for his engraved Cross pen (the winning prize from a regional spelling bee some years ago) and began to write. As was his custom, he employed his left thigh as a makeshift desk:

November 13th

It will either happen today or not all. I've had my fill of thinking about it.

After making this last entry, George stared at the page for a several moments—his expression suggesting he'd just arrived at an especially jarring, perhaps even life-altering discovery. When he at last looked up, he noted that several contestants and their parents had strolled into his vicinity, and with an air of panic, he quickly closed his journal and stowed it in the inner pocket of his suit coat.

At length, there was a patter of applause coming from

the direction of the stage. It was a polite kind of applause, George noted, the sort that was generally reserved for performers who've flatted.

As George looked up, a girl, who was roughly his age, sulked off stage wearing a pink saffron dress and a pair of ballerina shoes. Blinking her eyes profusely, George came away with the impression she'd either *been* crying or was on the verge.

"That's Ruthie Everett," a heavily made-up woman sitting to George's right stage-whispered to no one in particular. She then turned to her juggler son, "She must've bombed!"

Ignoring the woman, George watched as the girl walked off with one of the stagehands, a balled up tissue between her hands. Then, without warning, he rose from his chair and followed after the girl. When he was within handshaking distance, he pulled out a handkerchief and despite knowing it was a beau geste, handed it over, "Here."

The girl stared at George rather obliquely. "Thanks," she said and took hold of the handkerchief. She then flashed a lipsticky smile that made George feel not altogether uncheerful.

"You're the whiz kid from up north, aren't you?"

They stood dead-center in the main corridor—the type of locale that not only congested traffic flow, but had the added effect of making George feel wholly exposed and inhibited.

"I don't know about the whiz kid part," he said slightly put off by the question, "but I am from up Tompkins County if that's what you mean."

"Thought so," the girl said as she leaned up against a

support beam. "I mean, I'm not in the habit of reading the program, but at least that's what I thought it said."

The girl standing before George was waifish and freckle faced in appearance, such that one might mistake her for being much younger than her actual age of 11.

"I used to collect them," George said as he took in the full array of the girl's freckles, "but after the first twenty or so I stopped for some reason."

"Me too," the girl said inching forward. "I think I still have them under my bed or something."

George looked to his right and left, checking for any signs of his mother, but, among the many passersby,' she made no appearance. He then gave a cursory look at a tray of fresh-baked cookies that someone carried past and turned back to the girl.

"I'm sorry about your performance," he said after a moment.

The girl blinked her eyes. "Don't be," she said matter-of-factly, "I'm not."

"But you were crying," George said incredulously.

"It's all an act," the girl said with a smirk. "It's all dramatics. I've been tanking on purpose for weeks. I want out."

George stood open-mouthed. "Out?"

The girl folded her arms across her chest and slouched rhetorically forward. "Don't tell me you haven't thought about it. I mean, a smart kid like you has to have at least considered it."

George frowned and looked away, his face making it abundantly clear he wasn't about to comment about the subject.

"I'm sorry," the girl said in an apologetic tone. "I didn't

mean to put you on the spot."

George paused for a moment as an overhead speaker crackled to life and man's voice gave out a series of instructions. "It's okay," George said when the man's baritone faded out, "that's just not something I like talking about."

"Look, George," the girl confessed, "all I know is that I'm sick and tired of the talent show routine. That, and my mother's an absolute slave driver."

George nervously shifted his weight from one foot to the other. He was unaccustomed to talking with other contestants, let alone one's prone to divulging deep, dark secrets.

"What do you mean, slave driver?"

The girl issued an uneasy smile: "Well she's not quite in *Mommie-Dearest* territory or anything; she's just, well, slightly insane when it comes to the talent show circuit."

George stared back, indicating he was in need of more information.

"She used to be a champion ballet dancer and wants the same for me," the girl said for George's edification. "She makes me practice three hours a day. Here, look at my feet," the girl said as she slipped out of her shoes.

As George glanced down at the girl's feet, he saw that no less than four toenails were blackened and that several of the toes were either misshapen or very badly bruised.

"Oh," George said and looked away.

"Don't be embarrassed, I'm fine. Or will be fine," the girl said happily. "I just need a few more screw-ups and I'll be home free."

With an air of cautiousness, George looked to his left and to his right, "Is she here now?"

"Who? My mother? Of course!" the girl said and did an about-face. "In fact, she's right over there by the punch-bowl."

In the distance, George saw a fortyish, auburn-haired woman take a sip from a small Styrofoam cup. She looked nice enough, but had a driven, child-in-training look that he'd seen so much of lately.

"So how do you do it?" the girl asked as though the words fell out of the sky.

George's head swiveled back in the direction of the girl. "Do what?"

"Memorize all those speeches," the girl said. "Recite them aloud. I mean I saw you in Harrisburg. That Lincoln speech had to be at least twenty pages long!"

"I don't know," George said dropping his eyes to the Berber carpet. "I just sort of take a picture of each page with my mind. It's not really *that* big of a deal."

"What do you mean, it's no big deal?" the girl said excitedly. "They say you're a genius!"

George flinched just perceptibly, "Please don't say that."

"But it's true, George. It's true," the girl said as her face took on a serious conjecture. "I mean we're all hacks compared to you. Hacks! Even my mother says so."

As George stared back at the girl the rims of his ears reddened. "You sound just like my mother," he said flatly."

The girl laughed. "Is that so bad?" she asked good-naturedly. "I mean, she can't be any worse than mine."

George shook his head as though there was a misunderstanding. "It's not that. It's just, well, I'm not especially good when it comes to compliments."

"Well, you better get used to it," the girl said taking a

step closer, "I mean you're about to win this thing. Everyone says you've got it all wrapped up!"

George glanced at the white handkerchief the girl was holding, noting that she didn't quite seem to know what to do with it. "Just once I'd like to be treated like a normal kid," he said. "Just once."

"Why would you want that?" the girl asked rather quizzically as a fresh wave of contestants passed by.

George reached over and, on a sudden but pressing impulse, pulled the handkerchief out of the girl's hand. "For the same reason you tank."

"No," the girl said shaking her head back and forth. "It's different. *I* have to practice *all* the time. I can barely walk some days. All *you* have to do is memorize something." The girl gesticulated with her hands, "I mean, you don't even have to practice!"

George turned slightly at the waist and took a rather protracted look at the crowd to make sure no one was listening. He then turned back to the girl and for the first time since they'd met, resorted to what one might call his "'professional voice."

"That's a faulty argument," he said rather professorly. "Full of red herrings, really"," he said as he stepped toward the girl. "What you have to understand is that the underlying reason is the same for both us."

The girl studied George's face and squinted. "I don't understand," she said.

For the past several minutes, the duo had been shifting out of the center of the hallway and to the side alcove, next to a water fountain. Just then, the girl bent down to the fountain, took a sip, and stood straight up. "So are you gonna explain it? Or what?"

George watched the girl wipe at her mouth and for a brief second, thought her freckles had multiplied. Less than three feet away, a female attendant was passing out name tags. "I'd rather not," George said. "Whenever I explain things, people think I'm crazy."

"Come on, out with it!" the girl said and punched him playfully on the shoulder.

George looked down at his shoulder and rubbed it. "I *said* I'd rather not."

The girl smiled an infectious smile—the way only a waifish, freckled-faced girl could: "Come on, tell me!"

George hedged at first, took a breath, and then said rather thoughtfully, "We both want to be loved for the singular reason that we exist. Not because of what we can do. Or what we can achieve."

The girl took a long, hard look at George and smirked. "That's the dumbest thing I ever heard!"

George looked at the girl and frowned. He was instantly sad, maybe a trifle hurt. "Look, I was trying to help you," he said. "To make you understand. It's not *my* fault if it's over your-"

In the next instant, the girl's mother began to urgently call her over. They exchanged a series of hand gestures and then the girl turned back to George.

"You'd better get going," George said in a tone that was sure to be a conversation ender. "I don't think we should talk anymore."

"Don't be sore, George," the girl said grabbing hold of his hand. "You're not sore, are you?"

George didn't say anything; his mouth was open, but only just. In the distance, he saw the girl's mother approach. "No, I'm not mad," he said finally. "In fact, outside of my own reflection, you're the finest friend I've ever had."

The girl crinkled up her face, giving the impression she wasn't sure if that was meant to be a joke. "Just remember," she said as though she was dispensing last-minute advice, "They *only* love us because of what we can do. Because of what we can achieve." And with that, the girl's mother put a hand on her shoulder and frog-marched her toward the exit.

"Five minutes, George. Five minutes," the master of ceremony said as he sidled past George.

The boy nodded, but said nothing, his mind seemingly lost in thought.

"Say," the man said as he stopped short and turned around, "It's the same deal as usual. The speeches are in a big jug. I'll just give it a good shake and pull one out."

George nodded, but once again said nothing. Inside his head, it was as though firecracker after firecracker were going off.

"Are you okay?" the man asked. "You look a little pale."

George gave the man a hard stare—his expression alternating between either killing the man or giving him a hug. "I've been cadet-like when it comes to this dirty, tricky business," he announced. "Cadet-like!"

"Are you sure you're okay?" the man asked as he tilted his head sideways. "Want me to get your mother?"

"Cadets need a break sometimes," George said as he stomped his foot on the floor, "We're just like everyone else!"

The man looked at George for a moment as if he wasn't entirely sure he'd heard him correctly and then backed away as though he had no intention of finding out. "Well, as I've said, you've got five minutes," he repeated and quickly hot-footed it down the corridor.

At length, George buttoned his suit coat, adjusted his tie, and then pinned his name tag onto his front-left pocket. He then marched forward in the direction of the stage lights. After making two sharp lefts and a right he arrived at the bottom of the catwalk staircase. With no one looking, he then climbed the stairs taking two steps at a time before arriving at the landing: "Thirty-five, forty feet," he said to himself. "Thirty-five, forty feet."

Atop the catwalk, George expelled a breath and let his mind empty out. Below, theatergoers filed in and out; his very own mother and uncle among them. It was a grandparent-sort-of-day, he decided—a multi-flashbulb occasion that would inevitably be time-stamped into many a child's scrapbook. In the distance, he saw two television cameras at the very back of the theater and next to them, a reporter who had interviewed him just last week.

Just then, at what was roughly a forty-five-degree angle, the master of ceremonies took the stage to a triumphal ovation:

"Today's last contestant is 8 years old. That's right, 8! He has appeared on several local radio stations, cable access channels, and been featured in countless newspaper articles. While the boy's talents are immense and his routine often varies, today he will recite a famous historical speech he's never laid eyes on word for word, after having reviewed it for no more than five minutes. Ladies and gentlemen, George Martian!"

George took one last look at his name tag and ripped it from his chest. Then, with a faint, fleeting smile, he gazed at his mother, erect and motionless. As he closed his eyes, he discarded all thought. Then, with but little pretext, he jumped.

CHAPTER 2: AWAKENINGS

The smallish-looking boy at the kitchen table in the untucked, Garanimal shirt gave his mother a quick once-over before biting down on a spoonful of cereal with a crunch. He then pushed the still-full bowl away from him as though the rest of it was unfinishable.

From the opposite end of the table, Mrs. Martian looked up from the long-distance calling plans she'd been sorting through and said matter-of-factly, "You'll have to do better than that, George," and without waiting for a response, went back to her papers.

The boy, in all his boyness, groaned aloud, but after a moment, two-armed his bowl and gulped down what remained of his Raisin Bran in one long, pre-adolescent slurp.

Mrs. Martian looked up once more. "I wish you wouldn't do that, George"," she said.

"Sorry, Mom," the boy said and burped.

From seemingly out of nowhere, an espadrilled girl in a butter-yellow dress entered the kitchen and, talking to no one in particular, asked, "Where's Dad?"

With no response from the table, the girl approached the kitchen counter where a variety pack of Kellogg's cereal and a bulk-sized container of waffles had been laid out. After fingering several boxes, the girl settled on a pair of waffles and fed them into a late-model toaster.

"I just don't understand why he can't ride with Dad," the girl said, nodding at her brother. "I mean, why do I have to get stuck with him?" the girl asked, addressing her mother.

Mrs. Martian crinkled up her face, indicating that the subject had not only been discussed ad nauseam but that it had long since been decided upon. She then turned to George and employed a tone of voice she generally reserved for when she wanted him out of hearing distance. "Do me a favor George," she said. "Go grab the vitamins."

George looked up from his placemat and blinked. He was unaccustomed to being charged with errand running and, as such, wasn't sure he was qualified to do so.

"Wh-wh-where are they?" he asked nervously.

"Think they're there on the bathroom counter," Mrs. Martian said. "Now be a doll and grab 'em."

"Okay," George said and trotted out of the room.

With her youngest out of earshot, Mrs. Martian turned her attention to her daughter. "First of all, Annabelle," Mrs. Martian said as her voice became slightly agitated, "your father has already left for work." She cleared her throat, "And secondly, the whole thing with the bus has already been discussed with you. I mean we *all* agreed on it."

Annabelle stared fixedly at the toaster. "*I* never agreed to anything," the girl said flatly.

Mrs. Martian pursed her lips. "Well, that may be," she conceded, "but you know as well as I do that Georgie can't manage the bus on his own. I mean, we simply can't have a repeat of last year."

As her waffles popped up from the toaster, Annabelle reached for a plate. "Just because he ended up in East Podunk and wet himself isn't *my* fault. I mean, *I* have to have some semblance of a-"

Just then, there was a creak of a small boy's feet on the hallway stairs. A fractional moment later, George lunged

34

into the room holding a bottle of pills between his hands.

"Here," the boy said as he held the bottle out for his mother's inspection.

Mrs. Martian leaned in close and squinted her eyes. "This is aspirin, George. ASPIRIN. You want the ones with Fred Flintstone on the cover. You know, the cartoon?"

George took the pills back from his mother and frowned. "Okay," he said and raced off once more.

Mrs. Martian pushed the papers that were in front of her to the center of the table. "Look, Annabelle," she said as she tried reasoning with her daughter, "your father and I ask a lot of you. We know that. But we don't really have a choice. I mean it's not as if *I* can get on the bus with him."

Annabelle sat down at the kitchen table and proceeded to pour a spangle of maple syrup over her waffles (ever since reading a magazine article entitled, "Are Condiments Killing Your Figure?" she'd been preoccupied with her eating habits). It was, of course, all part of her newfound "boy phase"," a sudden and all-encompassing desire to be gym-fit and prettied up. It was the kind of thing her father liked to tease her about, one of the myriad jokes that George would not and could not "get." As Annbelle gripped the bottle of Aunt Jemima by the throat, she shot her mother a propulsive stare.

"Are you ever going to tell George that he had an accident? I mean, are you and Dad ever going to tell him that he isn't the same as he used to be?" Annabelle asked. "I mean, he fell nearly thirty feet and all, and I just think he should know," the girl said matter-of-factly."

Mrs. Martian angled her head down at the table, expelled a breath, and then brought her head back up again. "Your father and I don't think he's ready, Annabelle," she said rather breathlessly. "Besides, nobody can really find anything wrong with him. I mean, he stutters now and then and his head is always in the clouds, but beyond that nobody could really say for sure. In fact, Dr. Strauss even said that we may never know."

Annabelle set down her plate and sidled up to her mother. Then with the efficient, clear-headed thinking of a perennial debate-team champion, she said, "What do you mean, we may never know? He *was practically* a genius. I mean, how many 5-year-olds could memorize the Emancipation Proclamation in a matter of minutes and then recite whole damn thing word for word? Huh, Ma? Huh?"

Just then, George reentered the kitchen holding a bottle of Flintstone vitamins and, as he approached his mother, he rattled the bottle in a sort celebratory fashion. As he set the bottle down before his mother, he had the vague feeling that he'd been the topic of conversation.

"Thanks, Georgie," Mrs. Martian said as she opened up the bottle. "Here," she said and handed him two vitamins.

George swallowed the chewable pills and then looked over at this sister. "Hey," he said, "wha-wha-what were you guys ta-ta-talking about?"

Mrs. Martian stood up from the table, "Nothing, George. Your sister and I were just going over the bus arrangements." Mrs. Martian took a sip of saccharine-laced coffee. "She's going to sit right next to you on the bus this year."

George scratched his head. "I thought she was r-r-riding the big kid's bus this year."

"Well, she *was*," Mrs. Martian said diplomatically, "but we just wanted to make sure you get to school okay. "Isn't that right Annabelle?"

Annabelle flashed her mother a faintly hostile look and then turned towards her brother. "Yes, George, 'it's true. I'm riding with you All YEAR LONG," she said, emphasizing her last three words. "In fact, I may forgo ninth grade altogether just so I can be your very own personal escort." And without waiting for a reply, she stormed out of the room.

George stared blankly at the back of his sister's head and shrugged. He had the vague notion she was upset by something, but he wasn't sure exactly what. He thought he could remember a time when things made more sense, but that part of his mind seemed to be gone, was never there, or was useless.

As George stood in a kind of torpid spectation he felt more like a camera than an actual participant. "Finish your juice, George," he heard his mother say as she chased after Annabelle, "I'll be right back."

With the kitchen to himself, George reached over and turned on a small black-and-white TV, and as it hummed to life, the screen flickered as though in want of more amperage. Taking a half step closer, George adjusted the rabbit ears (the Martians were notorious cable TV holdouts), until the channel cleared up and a cartoon that he recognized, but could not remember the name of, appeared. He then sat down, picked up his glass of pulpless juice, and compliantly drank if off.

Some fifteen minutes later, Mrs. Martian returned to the kitchen, her face suggesting that she'd just had a long, rather unpleasant conversation with her eldest child. As she stepped through the doorway of her recently remodeled slate-floor kitchen, her reentry was not only physical, but verbal—for she appeared to be in midst of muttering to herself. It was not the prototypical housewifely mutterings of a Reaganite-era mother of two, but rather the pent-up grievances (outcries, really) of a mother forever trying to reconcile the needs of an all-American, simon-pure daughter with those of a once-great, near-genius son, who had now been rendered something far, far less.

As George eyed his mother, her movements had a violent, warlike quality, so much so that for several minutes he was afraid to even speak. When he at last worked up the requisite nerve, he did his best to come across as a noncombatant. "Wha-wha-where's Annabelle?"

Mrs. Martian dropped her pen and interdigitated her hands. "That's hard to say, George," she said in a voice loud enough for anyone in the house to hear. "She may be in any number of places: in her *precious* bedroom, taking *yet another* bath, or maybe even packing her bags for greener pastures!"

George set both elbows on the edge of the table, his mind a flurry of slow-churned afterthoughts. "Is she still going with me on the bus?"

Mrs. Martian looked at her receptive audience, but made no reply. It was as though the very question was somehow altogether unanswerable.

"Listen, George," Mrs. Martian said as she leaned forward and wiped away a bit of sleep in his eye. "Your sister is getting to the point where she wants to be with her friends. I mean, she wants to help you and all, it's just that, well, when you get to ninth grade, you don't always want to pal around with fourth graders, understand?"

George squinted his eyes as though he was in need

more of clarification. "But is she going with me on the bus?"

Mrs. Martian forced a smile, "Well, the thing is, George, I can't exactly-"

Just then, the now jean-jacketed girl in question poked her head in the door. "Come on, George," she said, making a point to not look at her mother. "Let's go!" And before there was a chance to respond, the front door opened and just as quickly slammed shut.

Mrs. Martian closed her eyes and expelled a long, breath. "Well, there's your answer. Now go get your book bag. The bus'll be here soon."

Annabelle Martian stood on the slight downslope at the end of her driveway with her family's two-toned mailbox an arm's length away. Behind her, the early-morning sun was making a surprise, cameo appearance. Streetward, her brother George had for about the fifth or sixth time drifted into the center of the road, and so, in a tone of voice that was intended to be both caviling and bitchy she said, "Hey, dipshit! Outta the road. Now!"

Her listenership scuffed his Velcroed sneakers on the macadam, but made no reply. Instead, he reached down and picked up a small, roundish object from the road that was caked with dirt on both sides.

"Put that down," Annabelle said with mounting irritation. "It's filthy!"

From a crouched position, George looked over in the general direction of his sister. "I think it's a bike reflector," he said waving the object. "Dad must've thought it was garabage when he put the trash out!""

Annabelle took a step closer. "Wonderful, George.

Wonderful. Now how 'bout getting out of the road?" she said as she gave her Dorothy Hammill haircut a needless adjustment.

George stood up, but lingered as though the spot where he'd found the object was a rendezvous point of some kind. "Must've lost it the other night," he said to himself and ambled over to his sister.

"Well, goody for you, George," Annabelle said sarcastically as she watched her brother use his thumbnail to scrape dirt off the object. "Goody for you."

The Martian children fell silent for the next few moments as though the rigor of the first day of school had already begun to take its unenviable toll. Across the street, a garage door opened, and a little farther down, from some indiscernible point, a dog began to bark.

"So," George said rather abruptly as he adjusted his book bag in the one-shoulder strap method, "when's our bus coming?"

Annabelle expelled a long, inhospitable sigh and then looked down at her brother's head as though the very question were somehow unpardonable. "Listen, George. If you're gonna ask dumb questions, you might as well not say *anything*. I mean, how exactly am *I* supposed to know when the bus is coming, huh?"

George gazed at his sister with his mouth slacked open, a gob of drool hanging rather precariously from his chin. "S-S-Sorry," he said like a master apologist. "I j-j-just thought you w-w-would know."

"I don't, George. I don't!" Annabelle snapped. "Now quit stuttering and leave me alone!" Annabelle turned her back to George as though she was done talking, but in the next instant, swiveled to face him once more. "I mean, for

God's sake," she vented, "do you any idea how much of a burden you are? Not to mention what a giant, and I mean GIANT embarrassment you've become! I mean, it's gotten to the point where I can't even bring any friends around," she said, and with that, she abruptly and with finality turned her back.

George stared at the nape of his sister's neck for several seconds fighting off what felt like a waterfall of impending tears. When he could hold out no more he abruptly plunked down on the morning-wet grass, Indian-style, and let it out.

"Stop crying, willya?" Annabelle said unpleasantly from a point just over his left shoulder.

George bowed his head and, with a quick, perfunctory movement of his hand, wiped at his eyes. "I can't," he said. "I just can't."

"Well, you'd better," Annabelle said with authority. "If the kids on the bus see you like that, you're toast."

George took a deep breath and tried to relax. He knew his sister was only trying to help, but wished she could be a little nicer about it. As he brushed a stray piece of grass off his pantcuffs he glanced back at his house: it was a five-bedroom Tudor job—the only house he'd ever lived in, and there, in the screen-door window, was his mother: peering, rubbernecking as if monitoring his every move.

At length, a wood-paneled station wagon came over the crest of the hill and rode past, only to stop mid-street and reverse back in their direction. Donald Pugh, age 46, shifted the car into park and, wearing his customary faculty button-down, peered out the window, offering a neighborly lean-and-wave:

"Hey, Annabelle. Hey, Georgie," the man said pleasantly.

George, who'd been preoccupied with the object in his hand, opened his mouth to speak, but before he could get the words out, his sister cut him off:

"Hi, Mr. Pugh," Annabelle said employing her best teacher's pet inflection. "I didn't know *you* were back in town. Thought you moved."

Donald Pugh reached over and turned the volume down on his car's radio. "No, I took a sabbatical. Spent a year in Costa Rica."

Annabelle squinted her eyes as though in deep thought and then opened them up: "Central America, right?"

"Yes, very good Annabelle! Very good," Pugh said, adjusting his seatbelt. "So you guys ready for school?"

"Sure," Annabelle said with a bit too much gusto. "Can't wait!"

"How 'bout you, George? All ready?" Pugh asked, again adjusting his seatbelt.

George stared fixedly at the man for a few seconds, trying to decide whether this was somehow a trick question. He'd never had Mr. Pugh as a teacher, but had a vague recollection of seeing him at some bygone school function. As he consulted what remained of the rather tattered Rolodex of his mind, he suddenly felt his sister poke him in the ribs.

"George! Mr. Pugh asked you a question."

George looked up from his sneakers and blinked. "S-S-Sure," he mumbled addressing Pugh. "G-G-Got a new backpack and everything," he managed to say as he held up a royal-blue number.

Pugh gave him an approving thumbs up and smiled. "Say, George, how's the talent show circuit? I haven't seen you in the paper lately. Thought I'd see you on TV by now or maybe the big screen."

George looked over at his sister and flashed a look of universal helplessness. He could never understand why he was always caught off guard by other people's' questions. "T-T-Talent s-s-show?"

"He's not doing them anymore," Annabelle quickly interjected.

Pugh set his forearm on the edge of the open car window, "Really? No more talent shows? How come?"

"Oh, I mean, he's just taking a break is all," Annabelle said a bit too casually as her face reddened. "Just a little break."

"Well that's good," Pugh said as he reached out the window and gave George a playful little punch on his arm. "Wouldn't want the boy genius here to waste his talent," Pugh said cheerfully.

George looked at Pugh and then at his sister. "B-B-Boy genius?"

Just then, from a point behind the Martian children, the front door of their house clicked open: Mrs. Martian then stepped out on the front porch waving Annabelle's pinkish lunch box just above her right shoulder, the hem of her bathrobe flapping immodestly in the breeze.

"Think you forgot your lunch," Pugh said to Annabelle as he waved to Mrs. Martian. "That is unless George has a pink lunch box," Pugh said with a chuckle.

"No, that's mine," Annabelle said with a smile. "I'll be right back, George," she said after a moment. "I'll only be a second."

George nodded but said nothing as he watched Annabelle hotfootit back up to the house. In the distance, he thought he could hear the elephant-like rumble of a bus.

Pugh shifted his car into drive, but it remained idle. "You know, George," he said leaning out the window, "*I* was the one who discovered you."

"D-D-Discovered me?" George said, looking up from his shoes.

"Yeah, George. *I* was the one who figured you a whiz kid," Pugh said proudly. "A prodigy. Do you remember that, George? Huh? Do you remember?"

George glanced back over his shoulder, noting his sister had just reached her mother on the front steps. He then turned back toward Pugh. "No," he said, baffled by the question, "I- I don't remember *any* of that."

"It was the craziest thing I'd ever seen," Pugh said as his voice suddenly became nostalgic. "You were only about 4 and there you were, sprawled out on the library floor reciting MLK's "I Have a Dream" speech," word for word. By God, word for word!"

George crinkled up his face, indicating he had no idea what Pugh was talking about. Behind him, his sister made her way back down the pavement. "MLK?" he asked.

"You'd pulled about twenty books off the shelf," Pugh continued as though he hadn't heard George's question. "And when I came over to you, you just started reciting speech right and after speech. Word for word! Without so much as even glancing at a book. "I swear to God," Pugh said, brushing a strand of hair out of eyes, "it was the craziest thing I ever saw!"

George stood for a moment, digesting what was for him, breaking news. As he opened his mouth to speak, his sister appeared behind him.

"Well, I'm glad you didn't forget your lunch," Pugh said, addressing Annabelle.

"Me too," Annabelle with just the right amount of apple-polish in her voice. "I *hate* school lunches."

"I don't blame you," Pugh agreed and in a commiserating fashion held up a small, brown lunch bag.

As George shifted his weight from one foot to another, an alarm on Pugh's wristwatch abruptly sounded causing him to visibly flinch.

"Sorry, guys," Pugh said as he fumbled with a button on the side the watch. "I gotta go. Can't exactly be late on the first of day school. But listen," he said as the alarm stopped, "have a swell day!"

"You, too," Annabelle said with a grin. She then turned to George, "Say goodbye, George."

George looked up from his scraping routine and said "Bye, Mr. Pugh." And with that, Pugh revved the engine and pulled into the street.

As the Martian children watched Pugh leave, the morning sun became hot over the front lawn and abruptly, familiarly, they were at once unshadowed.

"*I* used to be in talent shows?" George asked abruptly as he turned to face his sister. "*I* was a whiz kid?"

Annabelle glanced back at her house and bit her bottom lip. "Never mind that, George," she said dismissively. "Mr. Pugh was just being silly."

George crinkled up his face as though he was in deep thought. Inside his head, he muscled at some distant, bygone memory. "No, he wasn't," he said after a moment. "I think I remember. I used to memorize speeches. *I* used to be in contests," he said proudly.

Annabelle looked down at her brother and sighed. "Listen, George," she said, "I *already* told you. Mr. Pugh was just being silly."

George glanced down at the object he'd been thoughtlessly scraping and, with renewed interest, saw that it wasn't a bike reflector at all, but rather a medallion. As he squinted his eyes, there seemed to be something inscribed on it. Leaning in close, it suddenly all became clear to him:

"No," he said with newfound authority, "he was *not* being silly. *He* was telling the truth." And then for emphasis, he opened up his eyes widely and added, "I know!"

"Oh yeah? How?" Annabelle asked, unable to hide her amusement.

Without warning, George held up the object he'd found earlier in the road. "This is mine, isn't it?" he said unrhetorically. "Look, I took off all the dirt. It's not a bike reflector. It's a medal. It says first place. It's mine, isn't' it? I won first place!"

Annabelle again looked back her house, but her mother was nowhere in sight. "Yes, George. It's yours," she said dabbing the wet from her eyes. "You *used* to be a genius, George. An absolute whiz kid. But not just with speeches George, everything."

George looked up at his sister and scratched his head. There was a glint of sunshine coming off her recently pierced ears. "But I'm not anymore?"

Annabelle shook her head back and forth in a somberly fashion. "You fell, George," she said with an air of secrecy. "You had a stupid accident. You fell from a stupid balcony or something, and well, now you're not the same."

George was quiet for several seconds: inside his head, faulty synapse after faulty synapse misfired, a sort of mental chain reaction of a prodigy gone bad. At times he could feel tiny pangs of enlightenment as though the grey matter of his mind were muscling, inching its way toward clarity. "So, I'm dumb now, huh? Is that it?"

"No, George," Annabelle said delicately. "You're *not* dumb. It's just that you *used* to be super-smart. . . . I don't know, maybe even a genius."

George licked his lips and swallowed. Inside the engine room that was his mind came a flurry of vague memories, fragmentary moments of being celebrated and ballyhooed: first-place trophies and medals; standing ovations, encores, curtain calls. But above it all, that thing most sacred: the untellable devotion of one's parents—love.

As George studied his sister's face, he searched for something small, pocket-sized—a cantlet of hope somewhere, nowhere, on the two little islands of makeup that covered her cheeks. "And now?"

Annabelle frowned and with all manner of aplomb said, "You're something less."

"Much less?" George asked as though he already knew the answer.

"Yes, George," Annabelle said in a tone of voice reserved for delivering bad news, "much less."

Bus 14 dieseled forward and then pulled curbside. As George took a step, his Velcroed sneakers made a thudless, lonesome sound, but unlike the harried thoughts piloting his mind, it was a cadence all his own.

CHAPTER 3: FALL MIXER

It was the first big event on Prosper Middle' School's calendar—*The Fall Mixer*. To the dismay of Mr. Archibald (P.E. instructor and head chaperone), his gymnasium had once again been upended into a makeshift dance hall: ribbons, streamers, and the like adorned the walls, topped off by a mirror ball that he'd been directed by Principal Thurmer to hang himself. The mirror ball had come out of the general P.E. budget at the cost of $132 (a sore spot for Archibald and, to a lesser extent, the rest of the P.E. department, as they'd planned on using the funds on a refurbished pommel horse).

On the far end of the gym, just below a basketball hoop, stood the DJ. As Top 40 hits played, the tuxedoed gentleman's face was expressionless, thus making it impossible for Archibald to discern whether *The Fall Mixer* qualified as a career high or a career low.

As Archibald reached down and picked up an errant gum wrapper, he eyed the other chaperones on the opposite side of the room: they stood clustered together around a punchbowl in their prototypical do-nothing pose, and as he passed them, he waved with limited cordiality.

Before him, boys and girls milled around in the half darkness, only the bravest among them choosing to actually dance. Instead, most stood in assorted postures, hell-bent on not doing anything to embarrass themselves.

Mr. Archibald scanned all the childrens' faces, but watched one in particular: George Martian was five foot five, a short-tall by contemporary standards. His shoulders were small and narrow and did not quite manage to fill out the muscle shirt he was trying to pull off. At the moment, he was making a play on Liz Mooney, wholly unaware that the fly of his jeans was wide open.

Archibald had watched the poor sap make three complete loops around the gym, but opted to say nothing. After all, this was, for him, high entertainment. As he blew his nose on a monogrammed handkerchief his late wife had years ago purchased for him, he took a few steps forward, to be within earshot.

George stood shilly-shally before Liz Mooney, as though unsure of how to proceed. He then cleared his throat and employed his best leading-man's voice (he'd been the lead in last year's school play—a rather impressive Napoleon Bonaparte).

"So, Liz, I was just thinking, did you maybe wanna dance?"

Liz Mooney smiled back, trying her best to ignore her suitor's zipper malfunction. She was a good three inches taller than George, and her eyes were ever so slightly crossed. Still, if a vote were taken among the boys in attendance, on looks alone, she would have finished no worse than second runner-up.

"Sure, George," she said as she nervously studied her shoes. She then looked up, biting her bottom lip. "But I have to tell you something."

George expelled a sigh and, feeling as though the worst were over, replied innocently, "What?"

Liz stared at George for a moment, trying, rather desperately, to muster some diplomacy, but with George looking at her expectantly, she decided to just come out with it: "Well I hate to be the one to say this, George, but your fly is undone."

George looked down at his pants and blushed. Then, in one frantic motion, he abruptly zipped up before responding in a full-blown stutter, "I-I-I-"

Thinking quickly, Liz Mooney put her hand on George's shoulder, "It's okay, George. It's okay."

"But-but-but," he went on, addressing the floor, not the girl.

It should be noted, unparenthetically speaking, that George Martian, age 12 and 3 months, suffered from intermittent bouts of what his speech–language path-ologist—a Mrs. Barrows—privately referred to as a "machine-gun-style stutter." While all physical comp-onents necessary for smooth, unfettered speech were in place, something in the innerworkings of the boy's mind— a faulty synapse or two perhaps—caused him, on average of two occasions a week, to lose all matter of vocal control. While the instances had undoubtedly decreased, or to borrow a pet word of Mrs. Barrows, "abated," due to twice-a-week speech–language pathology sessions, she'd both personally and professionally resigned herself that no amount of intervention, regardless of the frequency, would purge it altogether.

Archibald watched as a crowd of no less than ten formed around George in a vague half-circle. While the boy's stuttering was generally a crowd-pleaser, Archibald's twenty-odd years as an umpire of bedlam sporting events told him that tonight's gathering was exclusively about the zipper mishap and, with that, he decided to sit tight.

George stood unreasonably erect, giving the impression he was, at any moment, ready to fight. Before him, eighth graders Tommy Griffin and Bill Shea pantomimed his zipper malfunction, going so far as to mimic his now famous pick-up line: "So, Liz, I was just thinking, did you maybe wanna dance?" At length, the routine devolved into a kind of domino effect as students of all makes, models, and serial numbers took a turn mocking him, zipper-down style.

"Hey, Georgie boy," Bill Shea said mockingly, "did those pants come with a manual?"

As George's face reddened, he tried to speak with authority, "Shut your trap!"

Bill Shea smiled and, with an air of ring-leader bravado, turned to those assembled. "Cuz if they did," he said with a laugh, "you would've probably read that a key part to wearing them is that, well, you have to zip up!"

There was a collective laugh, intoned with a distinctly juvenile quality, and as George's eyes welled up, he briefly wondered whether there was any chance his parents would allow him to transfer. Making matters worse, a wad of George's shirt (which he'd mistakenly lodged in his zipper) had made its' way outward, causing a three-inch phallic-shaped piece of shirt to stick out from his pants. Tommy Griffin, who'd been aching to get in on the action (and thus far upstaged by his buddyroo Mr. Shea), was the first to comment: "Hey, look, its Napoleon *Boner*-parte!" Seconds later, after a fair amount of persiflage and chuckling, the assemblage broke out into a chant:

"BONER-PARTE! BONER-PARTE! BONER-PARTE!"
"BONER-PARTE! BONER-PARTE! BONER-PARTE!"

Liz Mooney stood off to the side, feeling as though all

this was her fault. She would have liked to grab George by the arm and escort him—forcibly, if necessary—to a room, perhaps a kingdom all to themselves. Instead, she hopelessly looked on as George Martian, standing in the majestic shadow of humiliation, began to cry.

"BONER-PARTE! BONER-PARTE! BONER-PARTE!"
"BONER-PARTE! BONER-PARTE! BONER-PARTE!"

As Liz scanned the gymnasium for help, Archibald came into sight. He had a glazed-over look on his face, suggesting he was not, as of yet, inclined to intervene. The man's laissez-faire approach to fighting was well documented, and, as Liz nervously tapped her foot, she quickly realized she would have to step in. And so, abruptly and with great fury, Liz Mooney joined George in the circle. She then addressed Tommy Griffin, flashing her best scowl: "Why don't you be nice and leave him alone!"

With a smirk, Tommy Griffin looked at Liz and then to George and then back to her again, "Nice? I'm *never* nice." He then licked his lips and charged at her.

Archibald, at last, moved forward, almost as a slow-processed afterthought (boys fighting was one thing, girls were another). He had a condemned-looking expression on his face, which to those assembled, indicated that he meant business. Taking a spot directly in front of George and Liz, Archibald waved two fists, wordlessly informing those present to stop the monkey business. And with that, all manner of boys and girls scattered.

Archibald found George hiding in the boy's locker room. He sat on the bench, sour and inconsolable, feeling as though the entire world had only seconds ago betrayed him. Archibald blew his nose once more and took a seat opposite George. He wasn't in the mood for one of his speeches, but for some reason or other felt compelled to straighten the boy out.

"George? You okay? George?"

George nodded, but said nothing, noting that Mr. Archibald's nose looked especially large and fleshy, as though he'd recently recovered from a cold. He thought about giving him his patented don't-look-at-me-don't-even-talk-to-me looks, but seeing as how the man had just rescued him, he decided against it. The truth was, he was far too embarrassed to speak to anyone. Most especially to someone who'd just witnessed the single most degrading moment of his life. But as Archibald gazed at him, he knew he had but little choice.

"Listen, George," Mr. Archibald said in a post-nasal drawl, "You're going to be just fine. *Everyone*, including me, has been there."

Wiping a tear away, George replied, "Been where?"

As Mr. Archibald sized up the boy before him, he scuffed his shoes on the locker-room floor just perceptibly. While any number of the speeches in his arsenal would apply here, he found that in *special* cases it was best to tailor them.

"What I mean, George, is that everyone takes their lumps. Sooner or later it happens to all of us. Now granted, some of us take more lumps than others, but the bottom line is that it's not about the lumps themselves, but how you *respond* to them."

Mr. Archibald waited for a response, but none came.

"George?" Did you hear me?"

George looked up and nodded, but said nothing. He'd heard tales of Archibald's locker-room cheer-up sessions and their supposed magic, but had never really been part of one till now, and as he stared back, he wasn't sure he wanted to.

"Listen, Mr. Archibald," George said, "I appreciate it. I really do. It's just . . . well. . . . I think I'd rather be-"

Archibald smirked, "Let me guess, alone. You'd rather be alone."

Looking at the man with an air of wonderment, the boy made room on his face for a small but noticeable smile. He then nodded slowly. "Yeah. Alone. But how'd *you* know?"

Archibald smiled back. "Listen, George, I've seen many a boy make a fool of themselves. . . . Trust me, they *all* want to be alone."

There was a short silence as George grappled with this particular piece of information. It was the kind of statement his father would make but, coming from Archibald, seemed to actually have some merit to it. A fractional second later, the boy looked up as though he'd decided something.

"What else can you tell me?"

Archibald looked about the locker room for a moment, taking in the full array of boys-only décor. Amidst errant towels, deodorants, sneakers, and what-have-you, a seemingly endless parade of trophies lined the far wall. Nodding in their direction, Archibald at last spoke:

"What do you see on that wall, George?"

Squinting, the boy said, "I don't know, trophies?"

"Not just trophies, George," Archibald said. "*My* trophies. Twenty years of them in fact."

As George stared back unblinkingly, Archibald sensed

the boy wasn't following, and with that, he clarified: "There are state titles up there, George. *State titles*. Three in wrestling, four in football, two in track, and, by the grace of God, one in tennis."

The boy sat up a bit straighter, but was otherwise unmoved. Archibald continued, his voice slightly agitated, "Do you have any idea how many boys embarrassed themselves in order to get those?"

As George shook his head, Archibald answered his own question, his voice resounding as though coming by way of a large megaphone. "Hundreds! Hundreds of boys making mistakes. Embarrassing themselves. Getting laughed at, picked on, and what have you. And do you know what they did?"

The boy again shook his head, transfixed not by the man's words, but by his volume.

"They kept going, George. They kept trying. They didn't stop to feel sorry for themselves. They simply made adjustments and *made* something happen. And do you know what?"

George shook his head, a little afraid of the man. "What?"

"That's what *you* need to do," Archibald said. He then gritted his teeth and said with finality, "MAKE SOME-THING HAPPEN!"

Blinking for the first time in what seemed like minutes, George nodded and then, almost as an afterthought, added, "Thanks, Mr. Archibald. I appreciate it."

As Archibald wiped beads of sweat from his face, he suddenly rose to his feet. Ever since his wife passed away (by way of kidney failure), the bull sessions had become sort of an outlet, a kind of dialysis of the soul.

As he turned at the waist, he looked back at George. "Oh, and for the love of God, make sure you're zipped up." Then, he was gone.

In the parking lot, George stood apart from the others, occupied with his very own brand of introspection. He watched as cars pulled up one by one and kids piled in, knowing full well his own ride would be there soon.

In the distance, he could see Liz Mooney—her silhouette against the building reminding him of his catastrophic mistake. She gave a little wave, but he couldn't bring himself to wave back, and then for some undefined reason, he thought of what Mr. Archibald had said. Deep inside the boy's head, some previously dormant synapse began to fire and an idea began to form. Seconds later, George walked about ten steps, before breaking out into a full run. He then stopped short, nearly knocking Liz Mooney clear over. He leaned in close and kissed her on the lips. When he pulled away, he ran in the direction of his father's Oldsmobile, saying nothing.

CHAPTER 4: GET WELL SOON

On a cloudless-July-sort-of-day, George Martian, on something of a whim, interrupted his sister Annabelle's sweet 16 party by passing out cold. He'd been standing to Annabelle's immediate right and was about to help her blow out the candles of her birthday cake, when a guest, Evelyn Shatraw, suddenly became the victim of a rather furious nosebleed. Evelyn, a monumentally unhealthy girl, and thus accustomed to impromptu nosebleeds, managed to pinch the thing off, but not before a thin, unswerving stream of type O Positive raced down her cheek. George, for whom the mere sight of blood caused him to lose consciousness, proceeded to go chin-first into Annabelle's double-layer, vanilla-frosted birthday cake, smearing out both the "1" and the "6" as he narrowly missed hitting the edge of the Martian family picnic table.

The "stunt" as Annabelle termed it, inspired, what was at best, mixed curiosity among the girls in attendance. For despite being among "the in crowd" at Prosper Valley High, they too had long grown tired of little Georgie Martian's exploits: the night prior he eavesdropped on the girls as they played truth or dare, where from the interior of a clothes hamper he overhead Cynthia Haversack discuss a make-out session with one Roy Tarney, captain of the football team. At the breakfast table, George repeatedly passed gas (toxic in both odor and volume), causing his mother to send him to his room, "pancakes be damned." And only hours ago, as the girls prepared for a post-breakfast swim (the Martian's, by most upward-mobility standards, had a rather extravagant in-ground pool), he'd been caught sneaking a look as the girls changed into their bathing suits. (It should be noted that the late-blooming George, at age 13 had only a vague idea of what he was supposed to be looking for.)

Presently, George was lying semi-prone on a poolside deck chair, a damp, periwinkle washcloth draped over his eyes. Sitting opposite him was his mother, a breathtakingly domesticated woman of 46, who at moment, was looking him over with an air of parental detachment.

"Georgie? You alright? Georgie?"

From under the washcloth came a groan, "Ma?"

"Are you all right? Answer me."

The boy continued to lie silently for a moment, listening to the youth-quake of splashes and giggles that filled the pool. He would have liked to ogle the winsome beautes, the "girleens" as he liked to call them, but seeing as how his mother was present, not to mention already being in the proverbial "doghouse," he dared not take the chance.

"Say something, George," Mrs. Martian demanded as she leaned forward slightly in her chair. "I mean, for God's sake,' I'm trying to talk you."

George twirled the drawstring of his stars-and-stripes swim trunks around a finger and sat up straight. His mother's voice seemed to be working up to something, but he couldn't say what exactly.

"I'm fine," he said. "Just a little . . . a little run down is all."

Mrs. Martian reached over and held the back of her hand to George's left cheek and then pulled it away. "You know," she said as she studied her son's shirtless, hairless frame, "your sister's *very* upset. You're gonna have to apologize."

As George abruptly lurched forward, the washcloth fell to his lap with a matter-of-fact plop. "For what? Passing out?"

Mrs. Martian glanced in the direction of the pool where a girl in mid-plunge was doing a vague approximation of a cannonball and then turned back to George. "Look," she said as she crossed and recrossed her shaved-that-morning legs, "you ruined the girl's birthday party. I mean, do you have any idea how *long* she's been looking forward to this?"

George stared back at his mother as his eyes adjusted to the midday sun. Sometimes there was just no making sense of his mother. "But *I* couldn't help it," he said shaking his head. "You know I'm no good around blood."

Mrs. Martian issued a brief nod as though conceding the point. "Nonetheless," she said, "for the sake of . . . of family unity, you *really* need to say you're sorry."

George looked over at his mother, sad-eyed. "But-"

"But nothing," Mrs. Martian said firmly.

The boy expelled a deep, plaintive sigh and then dropped one foot over the side of his deck chair. He would have liked to employ his sister's patented move of storming off, but at the last minute decided against it.

"It's not fair," he said after a moment. "It's just not fair. Why do I always have to be one who-"

Mrs. Martian looked her son squarely in the eye, "I know it isn't," she said, patting him on the leg in a commiserating fashion, "it's just, well, it's just the right thing to do."

As a ray of sunshine caught George in the eyes, he made

a little visor of his right hand and squinted. "Fine!" he said loudly enough to give himself the upper hand, "but *only* because you're making me."

"That's swell, George. That's very mature," Mrs. Martian said with more than a touch of asperity.

George either didn't hear his mother or had just plain stopped listening, for, instead of keeping up his end of the conversation, he was gaping poolward: with his mouth slack-jawed and a spangle of drool hanging precariously from his chin, he watched (with a high degree of spectation) as a trifecta of girl-women applied about a gallon's worth of sunblock to one another's back sides. When he, at last, turned back to his mother, he slumped down in his deck chair and yawned.

"Where's Dad?" he asked absentmindedly.

"You know perfectly well where he is," Mrs. Martian said as her voice began to rise. "Getting ANOTHER cake!"

George bowed his head, "Oh."

"'Oh' is right," Mrs. Martian said, tightening the strap of her sandal. "I mean really, George. You've got to stop being so damn clueless!"

George sat back in his chair and put both arms on the armrests. "Look, I made a mistake, alright? It's not as if it happens all the time."

Mrs. Martian gazed at her son and laughed. "For God's sake, George, just last week you threw a baseball through the sliding glass door. What do you mean 'it doesn't happen all the time'? Of course it does!"

George again glanced leftward at the pool—this time eyeing his sister, who was in the midst of blowing air into a semi-deflated beach ball. He knew his mother was right, so he thought it best to change the conversation.

"What about Evelyn?" George asked his mother, as if remembering he'd been on the losing end of an argument. "Does *she* have to apologize?"

"Who?" Mrs. Martian asked as she rose to her feet.

"Evelyn Shatraw," George said, nodding at a girl wading in the far shallow end of the pool. "The bleeder."

Mrs. Martian frowned. "She's a guest, George. A guest." George folded his arms across his chest and struck a kind of big-shot pose. "So"?"

"It's very different," Mrs. Martian said defensively.

Two small flags of protest went up in George's eyes, "Oh yeah? How?" he asked sharply.

"It's just different, George. It just *is*," Mrs. Martian said as she retreated toward the house. She then stopped mid-stride and turned at the waist, "And we *both* know it."

As George sat listlessly, bikini-clad girls frolicked about in a kind of PG-13 movie-reel loop, and whatever guilt the boy may have only seconds ago harbored quickly vanished into a pool of hormonal ecstasy. Over the next ten-odd minutes, a panorama of girleen flesh overwhelmed him, so much so that very often he did not know where to look. At times he was partial to Elaine McCaffrey in polka dots, and other times it was Donna Grasso in stripes—but on the whole, the dozen or so girls were a photogenic, swimsuit-pretty bunch, and with the exception of his sister, would forever be picture-framed into the archives of the boy's mind.

The remainder of the afternoon may well have passed in the same vein if not for Annabelle Martian, who came bounding toward her brother at light speed. She wore a *one-piece* butterscotch plaid number (a sore spot for

Annabelle, as Mrs. Martian had not yet deemed her to be of bikini-wearing age). She was roughly ten steps away when George spotted her. Thinking quickly, he placed the now semi-dry washcloth over his face and played dead.

Annabelle stood over her brother with her arms folded in an unrelaxing pose. Then, with great suddenness, she reached down and threw the washcloth that covered his face to the ground.

"Quit gawking, you little creep! Haven't you done enough?"

George lurched forward in the deck chair, pretending to rub sleep from his eyes, all the while knowing full well he was sunk. "Huh? What?"

As Annabelle clenched both hands into fists, she spoke at an unprecedented volume: "Quit it, George! Just quit it!" She then nodded in the direction of the pool, "We *all* know what you were doing!"

As George stared absently at his sister, he wondered what was taking his father so long. A cake, even one on short notice, couldn't possibly be that hard to find. He couldn't say why exactly, but of late his father was the only one who seemed to ever take his side of things. As this thought and others swirled inside his head, he suddenly realized the entire pool party was collectively awaiting a response. He then announced, to anyone and no one in particular: "Well, I have to look somewhere, don't I?"

Presently, Mrs. Martian appeared, coming from the direction of a recently repaired sliding glass door. She held a tray of cookies in one hand and a jug of punch in the other. Her short, brittle hair was tucked behind her ears and as she walked, the makings of varicose veins could be seen by all. As she set the goodies down on an umbrella table, she gave her children (who appeared to be in mid-argument) a quick once-over. She then proceeded to clear her throat and, in her best kindergarten voice, said, "George? Did you say you were sorry?"

The boy looked up defiantly. "Sorry for what? Passing out? Yeah, sorry about that," he said turning to Annabelle. "I mean, yeah, guess I should've been a bit more considerate-"

Annabelle put her hands on her hips and snorted in disgust. "See Mom, that's what I mean. He's always such a-a-"

Looking as though she was about to rescind all present and future birthday celebrations, Mrs. Martian pointed her finger at her daughter in a war-like manner: "Don't you even think about finishing that sentence. Don't you dare." She then reached over with a high degree of drama and grabbed George by the chin: "Now you say you're sorry. Say it!"

With his head locked in his mother's vice-like grip, George had little choice but to stare at his mother: she was giving him her dyed-in-the-wool look, an amalgam of squinted eyes and grimace, that conveyed in no uncertain terms that she meant business. "All right, all right" he said loudly as he slapped his mother's hand away. "I'm sorry. *There*, I said it." He then looked at his sister coldly, "Satisfied?"

Mrs. Martian sat back in her chair, expelled a breath, closed her eyes, and rubbed at her temples. "Alright then Annabelle, move along."

Annabelle looked at her mother incredulously. "Move along? That's it? He didn't even *mean* it. Besides, he was gawking . . . at the girls" . . ."

With her eyes still closed, Mrs. Martian reached into the side pocket of her Bermuda-style shorts and pulled out a half-empty pack of cigarettes. "Enough, Annabelle."

Annabelle adjusted the seat of her bathing suit, "But-"

"ENOUGH!" Mrs. Martian grunted as she opened her eyes and pulled out a cigarette. "Besides, your father will be home soon. Now both of you, scram!"

As all parties retreated to their respective corners, order was in due course restored: the girls sunbathed, George napped, Mrs. Martian chain-smoked. Roughly one half hour later, the sliding glass door clicked open. Mr. Martin Martian then appeared, decked out in his poolside best: he wore an untucked gun-metal grey polo shirt (buttoned to the top) and a pair of beltless cargo shorts. In his hands was a cake. He was no sooner on the patio when he was nearly swallowed by a throng of 16-year-old girls, who not only happened to be at a birthday party but also had thus far been denied cake.

It should be noted that Martin Martian was, by all accounts, a swell guy—the sort of good-natured chap who could play kickball with his children by the hour, feed his neighbor's' cats while they were on vacation, and then, depending on certain events that were far outside his control, make tantric-like love to his wife of nineteen years. But if ever there was a person to foul up errand running (even when given a list), Mr. Martian was undoubtedly the man. It was never a question of intellect or Walter Mitty–type absentmindedness, but rather that while standing at the checkout line, he would arbitrarily decide that the product in hand was inferior to something else that remained on the shelf, and then, after several seconds of shoegazing, he would bolt from the line, exchange products, and inevitably arrive home with the wrong item.

While Martin loved his children, he did so from a distance. In accordance with the era from which he was raised, he left their day-to-day caretaking and domestication to his bride. He was not your classic, two-bit chauvinist, but rather a man completely and sublimely out of touch from the world to which he'd been relegated. Annabelle was, for him, a true and utter delight. A child for whom he could sit back and watch as highlight reel upon highlight reel of her life played out. But George was the rub. A boy who, more often than not, triggered the man's sympathy. And ever since the tragic fallout from the talent show finals, he regarded him rather like a small, injured animal, inundated by predators.

At six foot four and three quarters, Martin Martian towered over the partygoers, smiling at them almost majestically. He held the cake at his chest, and as such, no one outside of him could see the lettering. One by one—and sometimes in groups of twos, threes, and fours—assorted guests attempted to peek at the cake (tippy-toe style), but Martin Martian (in a bit of showboating) only held it higher.

Annabelle stood nearest her father with a canary-yellow towel wrapped about her waist. While she was not generally thought of as a demanding child, the late-arriving cake had caused her to give off a vibe of one who'd been denied a central part of the modern-day-birthday-party-type celebration.

"What took you so long, Dad?"

Martin Martian smiled at his daughter while George and his wife remained at the back. "Well, I had to have it decorated," he announced flatly.

Annabelle, awash in excitement, reached for the cake, "Let me see! Let me see!"

"Wait," her father replied good-naturedly, as he pulled the cake higher. Then with a broad, uninhibited smile, he said, "I want Georgie up here."

As Annabelle turned at the waist to face her brother, she expelled a low, just-get-on-with-it sigh. Seconds later, from a point just beyond her right shoulder, came her father's voice once more:

"George? Would you come up here? George?"

The boy stood on the slight downslope of the patio with his mother at his side. Moments ago, she informed him (rather unpleasantly) that he would be a non-participant in the birthday cake proceedings. When he'd argued, she'd gone on to say that the second cake had heard about the fate of its predecessor, and had, in essence, issued a restraining order against him.

With his injunction in mind, George turned to his mother with his head aslant and gave her a quizzical what-am-I-supposed-to-do look.

The woman, who'd been toying with the idea of lighting up her second-to-last cigarette, pulled her gaze from her husband's bullet-shaped head and with but little thought waved her left, free hand and said defeatedly, "Alright, go ahead."

After a brief, cautionary pause, George moved forward, almost furtively, all the while wondering what his father could possibly want.

"Hey, Georgie. How ya feelin', sport?" his father asked as he made his way into the impromptu piece of real estate his father had hollowed out for him.

" Good, I guess," George said sheepishly as the girl-women and his sister stared him down.

"Good, George. Good," his father said in a hospital-room voice. "You just gotta take it easy is all. . . . maybe lie down-"

"Um . . . Dad? The cake?" Annabelle interjected, elbowing George out of the way.

As Mr. Martian slow-motioned his head and faced Annabelle, a slight sunburn began to form down the length of his nose. "Apologies, Annabelle. Apologies," he said. He then adjusted the cake between his hands and looked his daughter squarely in the eye.

"Look," he said apologetically, "I know it's your birthday and all, but I thought, what with your brother being ill, we might make an exception."

George watched his sister's face crimson up and then he did a sort of reverse-thrust motion, backward. He couldn't say why exactly, but he had the vague feeling something was about to go badly, maybe even cat-astrophically, wrong.

"An exception?" Annabelle asked squinching up her face.

Mr. Martian glanced over at his wife, then to George, and then back to Annabelle. "What I'm trying to say, Annabelle," he said as though trying to get his words just right, "is . . . well . . . maybe I'd better just show you"."

As Martin Martian angled the cake for all to see, one of his children broke out into a wide smile, while the other frowned and ran off in the direction of the poolhouse. For instead of reading *Happy Birthday Annabelle* or some like-minded sentiment, it read *George—Get Well Soon.*

CHAPTER 5: CONDOLENCES

Martin Martian lay on the davenport, nondescript, and allowing small, uncertain breaths as his only sign of life. At his feet, in a violent, scattershot pattern, were mislaid throw pillows, an afghan blanket, car keys, glasses, loose change, and one upturned Populuxe ashtray—the ashes of which spilled out on the floor in a grainy, Dutch Master's rainbow.

From the innerworkings of the house, the furnace expelled an updraft of warm air. As the vent nearest the man blasted him, wisps of greyed hair rose and fell, but otherwise, he remained unmoved. At the urging of his wife, who'd recently read an article about a house fire entitled "Never Too Safe," he'd had the furnace cleaned, but had somehow gotten "steamrolled" (a pet word of his) into having the chimney done as well. As he'd written out the check in the "ghastly" amount of $412, his wife of twenty-one years patted him on the back and said, "Think of the children, Martin. The *children*," as the serviceman nervously looked on.

Opposite the man was an antique coffee table. There, splayed on the morning paper, was the family cat, Pepper. The fickle bitch gazed at Martin, her litter-box champion, with an air of wan foreboding, almost as though she'd been able to glean that the man had not only suffered a stroke but also that the blockage was of the three-alarm, intracerebral variety.

The feline's one-way staring contest continued for several moments, only to be cut short by the ringing of the kitchen's wall phone. By the third ring, Pepper vacated the first floor of the house altogether, leaving Martin (who remained in a kind of hypno-trance) to fend for himself. While he would readily admit at parties to not being a "phone man," even if his wife had been home, no amount of uxorial prompting could have persuaded him to move so much as an inch. For the cardinal fact remained that blood was filling the cranial portion of the left side of his head at an alarming, deathly rate.

With Martin Martian in a still, neutral position, the answering machine slowly whirred to life. A fraction of a moment later, as he struggled to remain conscious, came the reedy sound of a woman's voice:

"Hello, Martin, this is your secretary, Elaine Cavanaugh. You know . . . from the office? Very sorry to bother you, but, well . . . I . . . er . . . *we* were all just wondering where you might have gone. I have the folks from Kendall here, and well, we were all just wondering when you might be . . . um . . . back?"

As Martin Martian stared at the ceiling, he tried, rather desperately, to call out, but with exception to his own breathing, no sounds came forth. A mere hour ago, he'd still had something a voice, not to mention the rather freedomed movement of his toes.

"Martin?" the woman's voice said nervously, "Mr. Myer has just now informed me that the Kendall folks will be here for the next two hours. Their flight leaves at two. Anyway, please try your best to get here. Oh, if you went home to get your briefcase, we found it in the parking lot, silly! See you soon," she said cheerfully, and with that, the line went dead.

He'd arrived at the office early, pre-coffee as a matter of fact. As he'd entered the building from the rear employee-only entrance, he'd flicked on assorted light switches and unlocked the building's front door. Then, as he'd pigeon-toed his way to his office, he stopped mid-stride with a sudden, unprecedented need for some aspirin. Setting down his briefcase on Elaine Cavanaugh's desk, he'd ransacked the woman's desk drawers (she was a notorious pill-hoarder of all sorts). All at once, the pounding in his head that he'd ignored since morning came surging forward, nearly knocking him clear over. From a crouched position, he'd then toppled to the berbered floor, instinctively placing both hands on his head and hanging on for dear life. There was, at that moment, a parade in the man's head—a thousand pairs of booted feet beating down upon the pavement of his mind. He could almost see the band, in their cavalry-blue regimentals, marching forward at a four-count rhythm, his head throbbing, until he at last blacked out.

Some twenty minutes later, Martin Martian had wakened. He had a vague notion that something odd had happened, but nothing more. With his head a-pounding, he'd managed to get to his feet, two-armed his briefcase, and for some reason or other, wigwagged his way out the door. By the time he'd made it to his late-model Buick, a trembling melody of vertigo had set in, causing him to drop his briefcase to the ground mid-way across the lot. (It should be noted that Martin Martian had a strong aversion to doctors and, to a lesser extent, all members of the medical profession. There was no particular reason for it, other than the fact that it had been one of the familial-type idiosyncrasies his own parents had instilled in him during his formative years.)

The drive home had been a struggle, and he'd found that if he closed one eye he had a better chance of staying in the lane. With his hands at the ten-and-two position, he'd gripped the steering column tightly, but invariably one or other of them would fall off.

Two minutes into the ten-minute commute, Martin Martian had begun to sweat profusely, so much so that his skin had taken on a shiny, high-gloss quality, almost as though he was coated in polyurethane. He drove around the streets aimlessly for a time and even passed a hospital. At a stop sign, he had to jam on the brakes and narrowly missed rear-ending the car in front of him. With the car idling, he'd wiped at his brow and tried to collect himself. Looking up, he'd spotted a basketball hoop hanging from the front of a garage and below it, sitting in a puddle, was his son's tri-colored Harlem Globetrotter basketball. A moment later, Martin Martian pulled into his driveway. As he'd lumbered out of the car, the right side of his face was drooping and had, in fact, gone numb. After fumbling with the keys for several minutes, he'd managed to open the door, calling out his wife's name before collapsing, mid-stride, on the living room davenport.

A young boy entered the house by way of the garage door entrance. He had a distinctly unkempt, between-haircuts look, that unfortunately for the boy, would not come into style for several more years. Dropping his book bag to the floor, he looked about the room unblinkingly, noting that the Lego fire truck he'd constructed the night prior was in a state of disassemble (pieces were strewn about in groups of two's, three's, and fours, almost as though someone had intentionally smashed it).

As the boy stepped forward, he could not quite believe the flagrancy of it: he'd spent the better part of the previous evening assembling the thing (682 pieces) only to find that someone (likely his sister) had carelessly stepped on it. Moving into the hallway, he called out "Ma? Ma?" several times before remembering that she was not home, for she was taking the boy's sister, Annabelle, shopping for a prom dress. As the boy opened the refrigerator door and grabbed a juice box, he became vaguely aware that he was not alone in the house. In fact, as he turned his head, he could just perceptibly hear his father breathing, not to mention see the toes of his father's size-eleven feet. Leaning forward through the kitchen alcove, he said weakly, "Dad?" but as he gazed at the man, there was no response.

There seemed to the boy something not altogether right about his father, but for the life of him, he could not say what exactly. He had crimson hue about his face as though he'd just participated in a rather competitive game of who can hold their breath the longest. As the boy eyed his father suspiciously, the phone rang. Less than a full ring later, the boy picked up the line.

"Hullo?"

"Georgie? It's your mother."

"Oh. Hi."

"Listen Georgie, your sister and I are running late."

The boy adjusted the receiver between his fingers and swallowed, "Late?"

"Listen, Georgie, I don't have time to explain. Anyway, we have a few more stores to go to . . . can't find a dress."

The boy took a sip from his juice box, "Uh. Uh."

"Georgie? Are you there?"

The boy gulped, "Yeah, Ma. I'm here . . ."

"Listen, Georgie, I know you don't like being home alone, but your father will be there soon. Probably by-"

"He's home now," the boy said matter-of-factly.

"Your father's there? He's home?"

The boy grinned knowingly. "Yeah."

"Well then, put him on the line, will ya?" his mother said impatiently.

"Can't."

"Don't be difficult. Put him on."

George peaked through the kitchen alcove at his father, "He's sleeping."

"Sleeping?"

"Yeah. He's on the couch," the boy said, taking another sip of juice.

The boy gazed at his father speculatively, "Didja want me to wake him?"

There was a slight lapse in the conversation as though Mrs. Martian were contemplating this new piece of information.

"Ma? Didja want me to wake him? Ma?"

"No. Better leave him," Mrs. Martian said slowly. "Probably had a rough day. Those new clients were coming into town," she said absently. "Now, listen, Georgie, don't get any funny ideas. Let your poor father sleep. Understand?"

The boy gazed at his father and then at the phone. "Okay."

"Promise me, George," his mother said. "Your father works *very* hard. No funny business. Let him sleep."

The boy took another sip from his juice box. "Okay, okay," he said. He then cleared his throat. "Ma? Do ya know what happened to my fire truck? Cuz it's smashed."

"What's that? Your fire truck? No idea," the woman said dismissively. "Probably the cat got to it or something. Listen, Georgie, I gotta go. As I said, your sister is in the dressing room."

"Hey! Guess what?" the boy said excitedly. "I almost forgot: I made the basketball team!"

"That's terrific, Georgie! Just terrific! Your father will be positively thrilled. You'll have to tell me all about it later though. Your sister is waiting. Just remember, don't wake your father. No nonsense.. Alright?"

"Alright," the boy said and hung up.

As George reentered the living room he seemed about to address his father, but remembering his mother's warning changed his mind. Instead, perhaps only because he felt compelled to do so, he approached his father and, seeing an afghan blanket on the floor, covered the man up. It was the kind of gesture that in all probability was something the boy would never do, but today, on this occasion, he had the uneasy feeling his father needed something.

George hovered over his father for a moment, lingering, as though he would at any moment wake up. He wanted to tell him about making the team, of having beat out another boy for the very last spot. Staring at his father, George took no notice of the shallowness of the man's breath nor the pallor of his face; instead, his eyes were drawn, almost exclusively, to a wheel of his fire truck. The object sat atop his father's stomach, in the approximate location of the man's navel or thereabouts. While other, more astute boys, might have questioned how the wheel had arrived at this particular locale, George simply reached out a hand and snatched it up, his father not moving so much as an inch.

With wheel in hand, George sat on the floor, cross-legged, and proceeded to reassemble his fire truck. In a matter of minutes, he fell into a kind of Lego-trance and spent what was roughly the next hour two-fingering and three-fingering assorted pieces until the fire truck was at last whole. With the fire truck complete, George turned his attention to a Lego-filled cardboard box that sat to his right and happily began sifting through it.

All the while Martin Martian lay silent; he was powerless, not unlike a decommissioned lighthouse. In the last quarter-hour, his face had taken on an increasingly greyish quality and, due to a questionable throat reflex, bits of saliva were caked about his mouth. Yet despite his array of corpuscular failings, his son did nothing.

At length, the doorbell rang (Westminster-chime style) and George was jarred back to the present. Rising to a standing a position, he barefooted his way to the front door and opened it, not so much as glancing at his father.

The woman standing on the front porch was dressed in white and was holding a rather elaborate pair of women's opened-toed high-heeled shoes. She had a congenial, ready-for-a-long-conversation face—the kind that Lego-crazed boys have little patience for.

"Georgie boy!" the woman said as she grinned. "Your mother home?"

George stared back at his neighbor, "Hi, Mrs. Clancy," he said unenthusiastically. He wanted nothing more than to return to his Legos. "No," he said curtly and started to close the door.

"Wait a minute!" Mrs. Clancy said, raising her voice

ever so slightly. "I just wanted to give your mother these shoes."

George flashed a quizzical look, "Shoes?"

Mrs. Clancy smiled. "Yeah. They're for your sister, guess she has a wide foot like me," she said cheerfully and handed them over.

George looked down at the black pumps between his hands and squinched up his nose. They had a leathery, shoe polish smell to them and as George took a whiff, he vaguely considered handing them back over.

"Tell your mother there's no hurry," Mrs. Clancy said. "She can keep 'em as long as she wants. It's not like I'll be attending anything formal soon."

George nodded with limited gratitude, "Thanks."

"Say," said Mrs. Clancy as she eyed him suspiciously, "You're not home alone, are you?"

George squinted his eyes, "No, my dad's here, but he's sleeping," he said, slightly put off by the question.

Mrs. Clancy looked at her wristwatch and smirked. "*Sleeping*? It's *four* in the afternoon."

George shifted his weight from one foot to other. "Yeah, my mom said he had a long day at work and to let him sleep. In fact, she pacifically told me to keep the noise down so I should probably go."

Mrs. Clancy pursed her lips, in a manner that suggested she was a grammarian of sorts. "The word is *sp*ecifically Georgie, not *p*acifically."

George flashed a half-smile, "Oh, right. Specifically, that's what I meant. Anyway, my mom's not home," he said and again made a move to close the door.

"Wait a minute," Mrs. Clancy said. "What are you in such a hurry for?"

George opened his mouth, but couldn't quite broach the subject of Legos. "Homework," he said. "I made the basketball team and I have to keep my grades up."

"Basketball team! Well now, aren't you just on top of the world," Mrs. Clancy said. "Your father will be on cloud nine. Congrats!"

As George looked at Mrs. Clancy, his face brightened, but not being well-versed in accepting compliments, he averted his eyes.

Mrs. Clancy shuffled her feet, her white sneakers smoothing out a crack in the porch foundation. "Alrighty then George," she said after a moment, "I'll let you get back to your homework. Just make sure your mother gets those shoes."

George fondled the doorknob, "Sure thing, Mrs. Clancy," he said and paying no attention to the fact that the woman was wearing a nurse's uniform, happily closed the door.

A girl of no less than 17 entered the house carrying several shopping bags and was followed by her mother. Her overcoat, her hair, her shoes suggested that she was the sort who would win "Best Dressed" in each year's edition of her school yearbook. "Hello?" the girl shouted. "Could use some help with all these bags. Hello?"

Setting down the packages, both women removed their coats and then very nearly in unison, adjusted their hair. In the distance the clickety-clack of Legos could be heard, prompting Mrs. Martian to call out in the tired, wearied voice of someone who's been on an impromptu shopping spree far too long, "Hullo? Hullo?"

There was a patter of small plastic pieces from a distant

room followed by the sound of bare feet moving across hardwood floors. The cat appeared. As George rounded the corner, his now complete fire truck was raised above his head in a kind of trophy-stance, "I fixed it! I fixed it!" he yelled. He then stopped short at the slate-floored entranceway and eyed his sister: "*Somebody* smashed it, but *I* fixed it."

"It wasn't me you little twerp," Annabelle bellowed as she balanced on one foot and removed a shoe.

"Well, then who was it?" George countered.

Mrs. Martian glared at one of her children and then the other. Her pale, tired face looked more unphotogenic than ever. "Will the two of you *please* stop," she said and headed back out the front door.

Standing on two feet, Annabelle waited for her mother to be out of hearing distance and then addressed her brother. As was her custom, her tone of voice was such that she was not only dealing with someone of exceedingly low intelligence, but who was also losing IQ points by the hour.

"Look, Georgie," she said in a voice that was overtly condescending, "I don't know how many times I have to tell you, but *I* couldn't care less about something as *infantile* as your precious Legos. I mean why would *I* even go near the things?"

George frowned, "Well, then who was it?"

Annabelle crossed her arms and took a step forward, her posture suggesting she was ready for a fight. "What? You don't believe me?"

George shook his head and tried to speak with authority, noting that his mother now stood in the doorway. "No, you're lying!"

With her mother at her back, Annabelle cleared her

throat:

"It just so happens I do my best to stay away from the *damn* things. *And you should, too. I* mean, you're almost 14 for *Christ-sakes* and you're *still* playing with Legos?"

Mrs. Martian's plain-Jane almost-featureless face tightened. "Annabelle! If you don't stop this very minute, everything is going back," she said as she gesticulated toward the bags. "And when I say everything, I mean EVERYTHING!"

As Annabelle turned to face her mother, she visibly stiffened, but made no answer. A moment later, her mother commandeered the room:

"Now I want the both of you to listen to me," Mrs. Martian announced as she dropped two large shopping bags to the floor with a thud. "It's been a very *long* day," she said as she pinched at the bridge of her nose. "Annabelle, go and get your father. George, come with me, there's more stuff in the car," she said and, using her left index finger, boat-hooked George out the door.

When George and his mother returned, Annabelle stood motionless in the center of the foyer, all manner of color had drained from her face. In the girl's short, happy life, the expression she was exhibiting had only been witnessed on two previous occasions: when her pet gerbil had escaped, and last fall, when she'd contracted a rather unpleasant case of the Rotavirus. As Annabelle drew a difficult breath, she gazed at what remained of her family: "Daddy's dead," she said flatly. "Daddy's dead," and sank to the floor.

CHAPTER 6: THE CRYING-PARTNER

The master bedroom was dimly lit, its occupants awash in half-light. Heaps of dirty plates, glasses, and the like were strewn about the floor, lending the room a distinctly squalid-like appearance. Mrs. Martian sat on the edge of the bed, an unlighted cigarette in one hand and her dead husband's engraved lighter in the other. Her unshaved legs were crossed in a kind of three-quarter pose and her nightgown was badly in need of being laundered. Across the room, as though standing at attention, were her two children. Despite being in near-perfect health, they looked as though they were either coming into or out of a low-grade fever.

As Mrs. Martian lighted the cigarette she gazed up at her children. Then, in the clear, unmistakable voice of a woman who was not only heavily medicated, but had, in fact, lost her mind, she announced, "It's time children. It's time," and with that, they were set in motion: George Martian systematically moved about the room and turned on the three fans that triangulated the bed. He then approached the room's sole window and switched on the air conditioning unit. Halfway across the room, he stubbed his toe on a dinner plate before very nearly bumping into his sister, Annabelle, who, as it happened, had been in the midst of switching off an overhead lamp. They exchanged glances, but nothing more, and quickly joined their mother on the bed.

Their bodies lay casket-style, with Mrs. Martian in the middle. From a flat, supine position, Mrs. Martian took several drags of her cigarette before she reached over and extinguished it in a bed-stand soup bowl. Then, without so much as a word, mother and children clasped hands and just like *every* night, paid a formal call on God:

"God our Father, Your power brings us to birth, Your providence guides our lives, and by Your command, we return to dust.

"Lord, those who die still live in Your presence, their lives change but do not end. I pray in hope for my family, relatives, and friends, and for all the dead known to You alone.

"In company with Christ, Who died and now lives, may they rejoice in Your kingdom, where all our tears are wiped away. Unite us together again in one family, to sing Your praise forever and ever."

George lay silent as his mind emptied out. He could not remember the last time either he or his sister slept in their own rooms, let alone went without the bedtime prayer. As the nearest fan oscillated over him, goosebumps formed: carefully, almost surreptitiously, he adjusted the comforter ever so slightly, hoping the bed's other occupants did not protest, which, depending on the night, could be a tricky business.

As George looked into the blackness he noted the rise and fall of his mother's chest, and a little farther beyond that point, was his sister. For the past two weeks she'd been getting up in the night at odd hours and George had yet to figure out why. He'd been meaning to do a little late-night investigation, but had not, as of yet, worked up the nerve to do so.

Presently, as George turned his head outward, in a slightly northeastern direction, he could just make out his mother's chiffonier. There, in a pattern that vaguely reminded him of the Manhattan skyline (he had a poster of it on his bedroom wall) was a tower of assorted pill bottles. Over the din of his mother's snoring, George squinted his eyes and counted them, but because there were so many, he lost track midway through.

At length, the bedroom's AC unit (ostensibly set to 59 degrees) caused the temperature to drop to frigorific proportions, and as George tugged on the comforter once more, Annabelle sat up in bed and shot him a glare, thus informing him, for all intents and purposes, to stop the monkey business. A moment later, Annabelle abruptly rose from the bed and darted out the bedroom door. Even in the darkness, she had a wholesome after-school special look, but somehow came off as being overly hygienic in appearance, almost as though she spent the majority of her free time in the bathroom, which, as it happened, was where she was headed now.

Some twenty minutes later, George rose from the discomfiture of the bed: the absence of his sister made things out of harmony with the rest of the room. As he dropped his feet to the floor, he circumvented three dinner plates, a half-empty bowl of cereal (Raisin Bran) as well as several well-made German steak knives. In the small, narrow hallway George saw that the bathroom light was on. Encouraged, he tiptoed to the corner and found his sister going through the medicine cabinet. She wore an orange-and-white kimono-style bathrobe, which vaguely made her look like a creamsicle. On her feet was a pair of mail-order slippers.

As Annabelle closed the medicine cabinet door shut, she

turned and gave George a quick once-over. "What do you think *you're* doing?"

George stopped in the doorway before making a kind of reverse-thrust motion. He could tell she was in one of her moods, and as such, thought it best to address her from a distance, "Huh?"

"You heard me," Annabelle said as she stepped forward. "Now unless you were about to revert to your bedwetting days, scram!"

There was something overtly intimidating about her tone and as George averted his gaze from his sister's he instead focused on the frayed bathmat she was half-standing on. "I-I-I-"

"Quit stuttering, you little creep," Annabelle said as she folded her arms. "You can't go through life stammering for God's sake. Didn't that speech pathology lady teach you anything? Now beat it!"

As George fussed with the drawstrings of his pajamas, he started to turn away, but with a sudden dose of anger, faced his sister once more. "Why do you have to be so mean to me?"

Annabelle snorted. "Mean to you? Trust me Georgie boy, this isn't mean. I'm *trying* to do you the biggest favor of your life. Now go back to bed!"

George stared back, not quite sure of what to think. While he and his sister may not have been on the best of terms lately, he wasn't used to her being quite *this* hostile. As he studied his sister's personage, she seemed to be in secret possession of some object or other. "What's that in your hand?" he asked.

Annabelle clenched her right fist. "Nothing, George," she said definitively. "Now go back to bed," and in the next instant, her eyes began to well up.

George took a step closer, unaware he was moving out of neutral territory. "Why are you crying? What's wrong?"

Annabelle gritted her teeth and her brown eyes became very wide. A second later, she came at him, bayonet-like. "What's wrong? What's *wrong*? Are you *that* stupid?" she asked as she hip-checked him against a bookcase.

"Hey," he whimpered. "What's the big idea?"

Annabelle's face suddenly contorted into a maniacal expression. "You wanna to know what's wrong? Well for starters, Daddy's dead. And if that weren't bad enough, Mom's gone crazy."

Two small flags of protest went up in George's eyes. "She has not!"

Annabelle moved a little closer and let out a sadistic laugh. "Really, George? Really? Then how come she makes us sleep with her every night? Huh, George? Huh? I mean *he*'s been dead for almost year. And what's up with all the fans and the air conditioning? I mean for Christsakes, George, it's February!"

The boy bowed his head. "I don't know," he said weakly.

"Well, *I* do," Annabelle said as her chapped lips quivered. "She's crazy, George. She's crazy. I mean look at this house. Just look at it," she said as she gestured wildly. "It's an absolute pigsty!"

There was a brief pause in the conversation. George filled it with a series of high-pitched wails.

"Stop crying for God's sake," Annabelle said as she released him from the wall. "Just stop it."

George looked up, but the tears continued to fall. He wanted very badly for her to be his crying-partner.

Composing herself, Annabelle took the back of her left hand and reached down and blotted out her brother's tears. "You have to stop crying, George," she said softly. "You don't want to wake Mother, do you?"

George shook his head ever so slightly, afraid to break the momentary peace. As he looked at his sister, he saw that there were dark half-circles below her eyes and that her fingernails had been chewed down the cuticle, but other, perhaps more subtle, indications of a troubled girl went unnoticed.

"It's time for you to grow up, George," Annabelle said rather abruptly as she leaned up against an over-filled clothes hamper. "I mean, you need to start taking care of yourself."

George expelled a breath, and with his back against the wall, slid downward on the floor to a seated position. "Everybody always tells me that," he said as he wiped away more tears.

"It's true, George. It's true," Annabelle said as she tucked some object or other into the side pocket of her robe. "I mean, look, George, you're getting older. You can't go around depending on people all the time."

George stared at his sister, utterly confused, "Why not?"

Annabelle tilted her head ever so slightly as though she was choosing her words carefully. "Look, George," she said, "bad things happen and you have to be ready for them." She cleared her throat. "I mean, the people you depend on can be here one minute and gone the next."

George pulled at his earlobe, "You mean like Dad?"

"Yes, George. Like Dad," Annabelle said, matter-of-factly.

George issued a little perfunctory nod of his head, yet couldn't fully wrap his mind around what his sister was saying. "Yeah, but you're here. Mom's here. I mean, all the bad stuff has already happened, right?" he asked as he stared at his sister imploringly. "I mean, that's what Father Whalen told me."

Annabelle gave George a cold, X-ray-like look, "You just never know George. You just never know."

Just then, from some indeterminate point, came a rustle of movement, followed by the appearance of Pepper, the family cat. The creature sauntered its way down the hall, sniffed George's feet, and then curled up on the vacancy that was his lap.

"Do you remember when we first got her, George?" Annabelle asked with an air of one who was happy to change the subject, "Do you?"

George squinted his eyes. "No."

"She was a stray, George," Annabelle said as she pet the cat once, twice, three times and pulled her hand away. "She was practically starving when she showed up on the porch."

"She was?" George asked quizzically.

Annabelle nodded and then for George's edification went on. "Daddy and I used to throw whole slices of bologna to her, you know, when Mom wasn't looking."

George snickered. "Really? I never knew that." He ran his finger's over the cat's calicoed ears. "How come I never fed her?" he asked. "Why just you and Dad?"

Annabelle smirked. "You could never keep a secret, George. You *always* told Mom *everything*."

George shook his head. "No, I didn't. I never told either of them *any* secrets."

"Well, maybe you never came right out and said anything," Annabelle said with a laugh, "but your ears *always* gave it away."

George stared absently at his sister. He hated when he couldn't follow what she was saying. "What do you mean my ears gave it away?" He palmed his lobes. "What's wrong with my ears?"

Annabelle fought off a smile. "Well, there's nothing *wrong* with your ears George, it's just that whenever you try to keep a secret they turn bright, bright red is all." She gestured with her hands, "They're a dead giveaway."

It was an eyebrow-raising statement and in response, George issued his best how-dare-you-say-that look. "My ears are *not* dead giveaways," he said with a hint of resentment in his voice. "*I* can a keep a secret as well anybody!"

"Really?" Annabelle asked rather playfully as though she were humoring him, "Then how come Mom and Dad always knew when you snooped at your birthday presents? Or what about the time they almost took back all of *our* Christmas presents on account of your peeking?"

George looked up with his mouth ajar: inside the private screening room that was his head, he pictured the Christmas of "82 and there, in the afterglow of a streetlight, was the rather unsettling image of his parents threatening to load up the station wagon with all manner of Christmastime loot.

"That was *me*?" George asked in shocked amazement. "That was because of *my ears*?"

"Yep," Annabelle said with aplomb.

George bowed his head. "Sorry," he said in a mea culpa–type octave. "Guess I got us *both* in a lot of trouble back then. I mean I *almost* ruined Christmas."

Annabelle sat up a bit straighter, the laundry hamper making an unmelodic squeak under her weight. "Don't be sorry. You're a truth-teller, George. That's a good thing." She tapped her foot on the floor as though it was asleep. "Me? I'm a natural-born liar. Of the first-rate, genius variety. I can lie to anyone under any circumstances. I mean, I can fool anyone, George. Anyone."

George looked at his sister challengingly, "You can't-fool *me*."

Annabelle smiled. "Just wait and see, George. Just wait and see." The words were no sooner out of her mouth than both children fell into a momentary fit of laughter.

With his legs akimbo, George made a cursory look to his left and to his right, noting that the hallway was somehow different.

"Hey," he said, as the cat jumped from his lap, "where did all of Dad's boxes go?"

"Salvation Army. Came yesterday," Annabelle added as she fingered at some object in her pocket.

George expelled a deep, guttural sound as though he was in pain. "They took *everything*?"

"Relax, George. I put all the stuff *you* wanted in the basement. The war stuff. The baseball cards. Even the record collection."

"What about the home movies?" George inquired cautiously.

Annabelle frowned. "Yes, George. I saved the movies. But look, I don't want you watching them *all* the time. They're no good for you. I mean, how many times can you watch you and Dad play catch or take turns cannonballing in the pool? I mean, they just end up making you feel crummy, understand?"

George glanced briefly at his sister and then looked away. He could feel a fresh wave of tears coming on and, as a sort of counter move, wiped at the corner of his eyes. "Alright. I promise."

"Good. It's settled then," Annabelle said with finality and rose to her feet.

The gathering-up and eventual removal of Mr. Martian's possessions had been a sort of all-hands-on-deck family affair. The attic itself was impressively large, the kind of space where a lifetime's worth of belongings could quickly and easily accumulate. It was, in fact, the sole room in the house that Mr. Martian had complete and utter dominion over: a small warehouse of baseball cards lined the right side of the room and a smattering of vintage WWII collectibles, tagged and catalogued, were on the other. The sole furnishing in the room was an oversized hope chest that Mr. Martian, had years ago, commandeered into a catchall for his assorted video equipment, including, but not limited to, untold boxes of home movies. Mrs. Martian and the children finished the ugly business over a weekend—one of those raw, impossible times in life that are very much touch and go. The day had been laced with a certain unspoken sentiment—that the items handled no longer belonged to a father or a husband, but rather, through some trembling metamorphosis, were remnants of a man, his artifacts. When they were done, Mrs. Martian snatched her husband's lighter and left the room. Hours later, the children returned, each taking something without the other knowing, in secret.

Presently, as George watched his sister sidle toward the bathroom, he suddenly remembered why he'd gotten up in the first place.

"So why do you keep getting up in the night anyway?" he asked. "You've been doing it for almost two weeks."

Annabelle stopped mid-stride and turned at the waist. "To take a bath," she said curtly.

George furrowed his brow. "In the middle of the night?"

"Yeah," Annabelle said. "Between you and Mother, it's the only time I can get any hot water."

George stared fixedly at his sister: her face was so confident, her tone so assured, that he very nearly, if not completely, regretted asking the question. "Oh," he said after a moment, and then to make it up to her, added, "you can shower first in the morning from now on. I don't mind. I mean it's freezing-cold and all, but that's okay."

Annabelle stood in the doorway of the bathroom and with the exception of a yawn that was perhaps a trifle too embellished, her face gave away nothing. "That's sweet of you, George," she said, "that's sweet"." and And then, without so much as waiting for a response, she closed and locked herself behind the bathroom door.

A moderately attractive girl of 17 stood before a bathroom mirror, and after a moment of working up the nerve, disrobed. While her face in itself was pretty enough, her hips had preemptively decided to bow outward, as though anticipating that some long, arduous child labor was in her future. On the bathroom counter were a dampish-looking sponge and several dirty washrags. As the girl, or depending on one's angle, girl-woman, picked up the sponge with her left hand, she grabbed the washrags with her right and proceeded to drop them into a nearby wastebasket. She then pulled back the adjacent shower curtain and, using the sponge, began to scrub. An overhead light fixture droned in the background and, after several minutes of high-intensity scrubbing, the girl sat back on a green bathmat and admired her work. To the girl's right was an unlabeled cardboard box and, as she reached for it, she shifted her weight from one naked butt cheek to the other. She then gave the box a ruminative stare and, after a moment, dug into it. Inside the cram-jammed box was a stockpile of her late father's home movies: super 8's and VHS tapes documenting Christmas mornings, birthdays, pool parties, and the like. As the girl rifled through the box, she picked up home movie after home movie and, with an air of one who'd been working up to this for weeks, unspooled each video's reel of film from its casing. In minutes, no less than thirty-odd movies were deep-sixed. It was the last good thing she would do for her brother. A gesture on her part to save him from constantly and habitually reliving the past. For the boy's nighttime routine of binge-watching home movies had gone from curiosity to obsession and was thus tearing him apart.

From under the closed door of the bathroom, Annabelle saw a pair of feet, the toes of which wriggled at irregular intervals.

"Go to bed, George, willya?" the girl said as she deposited the remains of the movies in the wastebasket.

The toes flinched just perceptibly and then disappeared.

"I know you're still there, George," the girl said as she bent her head toward the door. "I can hear you breathing."

A patter of motion emanated from the opposite side of the locked bathroom door and a moment later, the toes, as though fessing up to their crime appeared once more.

"What are you doing in there?" George asked leaning an ear against the door. "I *thought* you were taking a bath. I don't hear any water."

As the girl glared at the toes, she pulled her rather longish brown hair out of her eyes and in a manner peculiar and generally limited to privacy-lovers, banged a fist on the midsection of the door:

"The tub was filthy!" she hissed. "Had to clean it. Now for God's sake, go to bed!"

"I couldn't fall asleep," George explained, his shoulder leaning against the door. "I was just . . . just laying there waiting to hear the water, but it never came."

The girl expelled a breath, rose to her feet, pulled a piece of lint from her right thigh, and turned on the tub's hot water faucet. As steam filled the bathroom, the girl reached over and picked up a large, unopened bottle of lavender bubble bath and, after struggling to break the seal, dumped an entire bottle's worth into the tub.

"There's your water, George" the girl said, addressing the door. "Now go to bed."

George stood for a moment listening to the untrammeled swoosh of water as it filled the tub. He had the vague, implacable feeling something was wrong, but he couldn't say what exactly.

"I'm scared," he heard himself say. "I'm scared and I want to come in and see you."

The girl opened her mouth, as though preparing to belt out a remonstrative word or two, but for some reason or other, decided against it. "George, remember when I told you that you had to grow up? That you had to start taking care of yourself?"

George absently reached down and wiped a swath of cat hair from his pajama top. "Yeah," he said.

"Well, this is one of those times, George," Annabelle said without any emotion. "Now you want to be a grown-up, don't you? You want to be treated like a big kid, right?"

George shifted his weight from one foot to the other. "Yeah," he said uneasily.

"Well then, now's the time," Annabelle said. "Now go back to bed right this instant."

Just then, the tub faucet turned off and the hallway was at once silent.

George licked his lips and swallowed, his unkempt hope the secretary of his mind. "Is everything going to be okay, Annabelle?" he asked as his voice trembled.

"Well, of course, it is George," Annabelle replied. "Of course."

George cleared his throat. "Promise?"

"Yes, George," Annabelle said impatiently. "I promise. Now go to bed."

George stared at the door, taking a series of little, small-boy breaths. "Alright then," he said after a moment. "Good night," he said, and at last turned away.

With the house to herself, the girl paused before the medicine cabinet mirror and, after several seconds, extended her right index finger and scrawled out a message. A moment later, she sank obstreperously into the tub. As she rubbed her shoulders, she expelled a much deeper sigh than was customary and pulled the shower curtain shut. Closing her eyes, she fell into a kind of Calgon-take-me-away moment and discarded all thought.

For several minutes, the girl was actionless as lavender bubble bath spumed up and over rims of her ears. Then, all at once, the girl opened her eyes and gave the item she'd previously stowed away a hard stare: like an amulet, the object went from one hand to the other, the girl making little windshield wiper movements with her head. Suddenly, with a look of marmoreal calm, she gave the door a quick glance and used her father's razor to slit both her wrists.

Annabelle Martian lay silent. The scene was very nearly filmic in quality, like one of her late father's home movies—the camera zoomed out, seemingly fading, when fading mattered most.

CHAPTER 7: THE GRADUATE

George Martian had a piece of cinnamon chewing gum in his mouth while he packed, and his jawline went up and down in such a way that it was difficult to tell whether he was happy or sad, bored or reconciled.

His mother sat to his right on a lemon-orange beanbag chair, looking like an intruder. Her face was caught in mid-afternoon sunshine; it did her wrinkles no favors.

"Honey, I could've done that for you."

"What?" George said, the word coming out all watery, like there was too much saliva in his mouth.

"The suitcases, George. I would've been happy to pack them for you."

George picked up a stack of freshly laundered boxer shorts and gave them a quick once-over. "It's all right, Mother. I don't mind."

Mrs. Martian reached into the side pocket of her periwinkle bathrobe and pulled out a nail file. "What time is the train again? You know, you could've just taken your father's car. He'd be happy to know someone is at least using-"

George turned at the waist to face his mother. "The train is at five, Mother," he snapped. "Besides, I've already told you: freshmen can't have cars on campus."

Mrs. Martian had begun to file the nail of her left pinky with quite some difficulty. "If you ask me, it's just plain silly. I mean, the very idea of your father's car just sitting here-"

George abruptly plunked himself down on his unmade

twin bed. "I'll tell them you said that, Mother. In fact, I'll file a full grievance on your behalf. I'm sure-"

"Don't, George. Don't. Or you're going to make me cry." Mrs. Martian set the nail file on her lap and expelled a breath. "I'm going to miss you terribly, you know," she said as her voice began to crack.

"I'm going to miss you, too," George said and quickly turned away.

From a distant room, the telephone rang, and Mrs. Martian bolted from the beanbag chair. She rarely left the house these days and so, with exception to George, the phone had become her primary connection to the outside world.

As George watched his mother exit, he tried, rather desperately, to regain his composure. He felt a vague sense of panic setting in, underscored by the fact that in a matter of hours, his childhood would officially be over.

George looked about the room and tried to focus on the present. He circumvented assorted piles of clothes, books, and shoes and approached his desk. Using both hands, he two-fingered a series of envelopes he'd been meaning to take a look at (the packing-for-college routine had devolved into a sort of all-hands-on-deck room-cleaning affair and in the last two days he'd managed to go through everything but the envelopes).

As George thumbed through the envelopes he quickly became aware that they were from some bygone time—a part of his childhood he either could not or would not remember. Just then, he heard his mother's footsteps. She held a tray of cookies in one hand and a glass of milk in the other.

"That was Mrs. Clobridge on the phone. She said she's

going to send a care package."

George nodded absently and said nothing.

Mrs. Martian stepped farther into the room and saw that George was holding ten or so plain white envelopes, each inscribed with a family member's name in large black letters.

"You don't remember those, do you?" she asked.

George turned and shook his head.

"Your father and I used to play a game with you and your sister. We would each draw a little picture, oh, I don't know, like an animal or something, and put it in an envelope. Then you'd have to try to guess who drew it."

George squinted his eyes at the envelopes and then looked back up again. "How could I not remember that?"

Mrs. Martian smiled as though remembering the moment fully. "It was a *long* time ago, George, everybody forgets things," she said as she set the cookies down.

George silently nodded as he cycled through the envelopes. He carefully inspected each one, noting that the ones labeled "George" were the only ones with pictures inside.

"Hey, how come mine are the only ones with pictures?"

Mrs. Martian smirked. "You could never guess correctly. If you guessed wrong, you had to keep the picture. . . the only way you could win was if you had an empty envelope."

George grimaced, "And I never won? Not once?"

Mrs. Martian fought off the urge to smile, realizing this was somehow important to George. "You came close, honey, but no, you never won," she said flatly.

Abruptly, and without the slightest bit of pretext, George picked up the stack of envelopes and tore them into halves, three-quarters, and eighths. He had wanted his last day home to be perfect, to be a singularly unblemished thing, but as he gazed at what remained of the envelopes, it had become abundantly clear that that was not to be.

"So I never won, huh? Well, you should've just lied to me. You should've just left me with the goddam illusion," George said rather hysterically. He gestured at the suitcases. "That would've made all this so much easier!"

Mrs. Martian gazed at her son silently, as though trying to get her words just right. She knew that he'd been trying to keep it together all week and that it was only a matter of time before things boiled over. "Georgie. Don't be like that," she said delicately. "Everything is going to be just fine. Besides, you win at lots of things."

George expelled a breath and wiped at his eyes. "It's good of you to say that, Mother, but it isn't' true."

Mrs. Martian's mouth tightened. "That's nonsense, George. Pure nonsense," she said as she tried to speak with authority.

George looked at his mother and gritted his teeth, "Bullshit," and sat down on the bed once more.

An awkward stillness fell over the room, the kind that is generally reserved for those who've lived under the same roof for far too long. George sat on one side of the bed, while his mother occupied the other. Each engaged in a kind of calisthenics of the mind: while George's psyche performed chin-ups and squat thrusts, his mother contented herself on a sort of introspective rowing machine. They were, in short, unlearning each other's habits.

At length, George rose from the bed and faced his mother, the springs emitting a high-pitched, staccato-like sound. Half a foot was between them, but it seemed like it was so much more, almost as though they were separated by some large, unbridgeable gap.

"I know you're only trying to help, Mother. I really do," George said plaintively. "But I think we both know the truth: I'm not a winner."

"Don't say that, Georgie. Don't you dare say that."

George motioned to the scraps of envelopes that covered the bedroom floor, "Mother, for God's sake, if I can't win at some lousy kid's game, what good am I?"

Mrs. Martian's mouth opened in protest, but George cut her off.

"It's okay, Mother. It's okay," George said as he raised a hand. "Oh, I'll be able to fool them for a little while. Maybe even for a full semester or two-"

"Stop it, Georgie. Just stop it. I don't want to hear such talk," his mother blurted out as tears cascaded down her face.

A moment later, George approached his mother and kissed her on the cheek. "Admit it, Mother. Just admit it. Besides, I don't think these cheer-me-up, milk-and-cookie sessions are doing either one of us any good," he said and left the room.

George stood on the open platform with his mother at his side. He looked glum, as though some event from earlier in the day was still digging at him. Of the thirty or so people who were waiting, none seemed to be the college-bound, matriculating sort. Instead, they stood in blue-collar, unionized groups of threes, fours, and fives, their conversations limited to the day's weather and the current price of gas.

It was a windless, late-summer day, the kind that did not require a jacket. Ticket stubs, Styrofoam cups, and assorted wrappers littered the grounds, lending the scene a squalid appearance. In the distance came the rumble of an approaching train, unleashing a flurry of shifting bags and feet in all directions.

George nervously scratched at his face when the train pulled in. He and his mother had said their goodbyes from the rather majestic view of the parking lot, but as goodbyes generally do, the experience fell short of the occasion.

George picked up his Gladstones when the train doors opened. He could feel his heart beating at an irregular rhythm. "Well, I guess this is it," he said, suppressing all emotion.

Mrs. Martian forced a smile, but said nothing. She then cleared her throat and looked her son squarely in the eye. "Now listen, I don't want you to be sad. I don't want you to worry about me."

George nodded as an endless line of passengers shuffled by. He knew that if he tried to speak now, his voice would be unsteady.

Mrs. Martian suddenly seemed to be struck with a rather serious conjecture, "You're a winner, George. You know that, right? I mean, don't ever forget that."

George stared back at his mother, his face casting a dubious expression. "Thanks, Mother. Thanks," he managed to say. "But I don't think we should pretend-"

Mrs. Martian suddenly made an impatient gesture and forced something into George's hand. She had lost faith in her words, in her once-great powers of persuasion.

George looked down at the envelope between his hands and opened it up. Seeing that it was empty, his face broke out into a wide smile. He then looked at his mother and said, "You and your invisible gifts," and boarded the train.

CHAPTER 8: LATE-MODEL CHILDREN

He hated them. The constant coming and going, the inefficiency of their movements, the graceless manner in which they lugged even their most graceful of luggage—and were it not for the ringing of the phone and the voice of the Madwoman on the other end, the entire scene before him might have belonged to someone else. Some other chump.

Instead, here was Gate C of Hancock International—aglow with lights and concourses, its' benches consigned to, or rather filled with, transients. There was Cowboy Hat to his left, chewing, George speculated, on something his doctor would have advised him not to. But despite the urge to reach over and wipe a swath of grease from Cowboy 'Hat's chin, George had his eyes on Polka Dot: a girl, a creature who, were it not for his present rage, would have inspired some very pleasant thoughts.

She was a string bean of a girl—one of those tall drinks of water who never quite seemed to achieve her full height. With flaxen hair and hazel-blue eyes, she was decked out in a periwinkle number, a frock really, and as George gazed at her, her beauty was almost impossible for him to define.

As he was about to affix her image on the scrapbook of his mind, George's view was suddenly obscured by Cowboy Hat as he rose to throw out his Styrofoam tray. And just at the moment when he should have retaken his seat, Cowboy Hat unleashed his best Midwestern smile on Polka Dot, and in a matter of seconds they were very nearly the best of friends.

He told her about marriage. How wonderful it was.

How at any moment his Missus would come storming up Gate C and into his arms.

As Cowboy Hat adjusted his Stetson, he revealed a blotch of Gordon Gekko slicked-back hair, a healthy dose of off-brand Brylcreem lending it a shiny, polychromatic sheen.

"Gladice and I? Been married for thirty-six years. Thirty-six!" Cowboy Hat said as he sat down next to Polka Dot. "We were high school sweethearts!"

Polka Dot nodded and offered some pleasantries, but unlike Cowboy 'Hat's booming game-show-host-like voice, George was unable to make out her exact words.

"Raised three girls," Cowboy Hat went on. "All grown up. About your age, as a matter of fact."

Polka Dot reached down to adjust the strap of her espadrille and smiled. A second later, as though her expression was a formal invitation, Cowboy Hat pulled out a stack of wallet-sized family photos.

Abruptly, and not unfamiliarly, George expelled a hostile breath and swiveled to his left and to his right, in search of the Madwoman. There were times when Mother called that he wouldn't even be doing anything especially pressing, but it was just the principle of the thing. How she always assumed he could drop what *he* was doing and attend to whatever crisis she was currently embroiled in. It was generally some small thing—some minuscule occurrence that her post-menopausal, widowed mind construed as catastrophe: she couldn't find the remote, had misplaced her keys, there was a funny smell in the basement. All these and more conveyed by way of phone— her voice intoned with all-out panic, demanding that he must, MUST come quickly. And he always did. Always. He was only too happy to mow the lawn for her or to put out the garbage, but these other things, these tasks, were slowly wearing on him; perhaps even killing him, like they had Father.

He'd reached the point that he now hesitated in answering the phone altogether, and if he'd given it a moment's thought, he would have done just that. But instead, he'd answered in haste. And now, here he was, waiting. Had he been able to get a word in edgewise, he could've just told her how to find the car: that with the mere pressing of a button on the keychain, the horn would sound, ostensibly leading her to its exact location. But after making "a hundred loops" in the parking garage and "not finding it," she'd lost any and all composure. He must come. Now! Drive she and Aunt Grencher 'round the lot 'till the car was found. It was the *least* he could do. After all, if he'd picked Aunty up himself, like she'd requested, this "whole nightmare" could have been avoided.

He'd been on court six, in mid-lesson, when he'd gotten the call—leaving him scrambling to find one of the other instructors to fill in. With one year of university remaining, he'd taken the summer job as a means of avoiding going home. For although Hillsborough Tennis Academy was only a few miles from his house, it required its' instructors to live on campus. Just the out he was looking for.

At times he'd felt downright bad about deserting her, of leaving her all alone in that big house. But once he'd learned Aunt Grencher was planning to "summer" with them, any notion of guilt had quickly dissipated. He kept picturing this horrific scene in which the three of them sat on the veranda drinking green tea by the hour, breathing in their assorted perfumes as they thumbed through back issues of *The Ladies Home Journal*. And that, quite simply, was something he could have no part of. After all, this was supposed to be *his* summer—the last of his true youth. And the whims of Mother, let alone a relative he barely knew, could not, under *any* circumstances, interfere with that.

"Sarah Lawrence," George heard Polka Dot say to Cowboy Hat as he rose from the bench and begrudgingly checked his watch. "International studies."

There was a melodic, sing-song quality to her voice and as George turned and gave her a quick look, he wondered if she'd once played the lead in some bygone high school musical.

"Graduated just this past May," Polka Dot went on as Cowboy Hat leaned in closer to her face. "Got a job at a firm downtown."

George pictured her sitting in staff meetings, aiming to please, her engraved Cross pen poised over a small of papers—her mind, her soul at the ready, sublimely unaware of the admiring eyes cast her way. She'd probably never even had a boyfriend, George surmised, but rather a seemingly endless string of dates: anonymous-looking men who were now, or at least formally, associated with a frat house, and had, for reasons they weren't entirely sure of, resigned to the cardinal fact that "dinner and a movie" would be *just* that.

Cowboy Hat shifted his weight on the bench and then adjusted what appeared to be a hearing aid. "How 'bout you? Big family?" he very nearly shouted.

"I'm an only child," Polka Dot said as George glanced over in her direction.

"WHAT?" Cowboy Hat shouted back, adjusting the earpiece.

Polka Dot looked to her left and her right as though gauging whether to raise her voice. "I'M AN ONLY CHILD," she yelled a moment later.

Cowboy Hat nodded and then leaned forward to show Polka Dot another, secondary set of photos. "Got a few more for you," he said with a grin.

With Cowboy Hat intent on using up all his spare time and that of Polka Dot's, George's interest wavered. As he ran an index finger over a dried-out contact lens, he *again* recounted his mother's exact words: "Meet at Gate C, right next to the customer service window." And here he was, yet *they* were not. He expelled a few sighs and once again scanned the crowd, knowing full well this would somehow be his fault: if he left without them, he'd be sentenced to a summer's worth of "how could you's?" and If he waited them out, it would be a serving of "where have you been's?" For Mother's sense of logic had become strictly hit or miss, and the presence of Aunty would only compound the scorn. He tried to recall the precise moment he'd become nothing more than a gopher, an errand boy, but found it impossible to say. He had a vague sense of once having been doted on— perhaps even cherished, but now he and Mother seemed bound out of obligation, saddled with no more affection than a tow truck pulling an ailing car.

All he wanted was his summer, with its criminal pleasures, with his days and nights uncut. But Mother kept getting in the way—kept calling him back to Weaver Street. It was as though something was knocking at his heart, an ungovernable brute invading his private sphere. He thought about mailing her an elegant ten-pager, a final bon voyage kiss-off. But the truth was he needed her. That the see-saw nature of their relationship would, with but a little a pendulum action of life, morph him from being needed into needy: just a singular man-in-crisis event and he would be in her arms. Thankfully. Maybe it was all those hotel rooms or the car rides. Or the brushing of his hair or the double-knotting of his shoes. The room service. The hours of prepping for interviews. But no, it was more than that, it was, it was beyond. For there was something in her motherly refrain, in her never-ending looped verse: *he* was special, a prodigy, a genius, a god-knower. Until you make a Christly mess of things and jump.

Over the next several minutes, George stared off into the distance as though dreaming of some other, better place. At the magazine rack, people stood in jagged swarms with their elbows nearly touching. They thumbed through dog-eared pages as a vendor darted among them, hell-bent on picking up fallen inserts. To his right, stewardesses, or rather, flight attendants, strolled by in the company of Clark Kent–looking pilots. He imagined them all having a drink together at the local Marriott or some such place— having a swell time, really laughing it up, all the while trading stories about flight school, maybe even snickering about chubby ladies who'd couldn't find their car. From over the P.A. came any number of announcements—flights on time, flights delayed or anything in between. It crossed his mind that maybe he could have his mother paged. But then again, in her panic, what was the use?

As George shifted his weight from one foot to the other, a large, rather outsized family began hugging one another in groups of two's, threes, and fours. He watched for a moment and then retreated to a bench, consciously sitting in even closer proximity to Polka Dot. She was still trapped in her sordid conversation with Cowboy Hat, but had managed to retreat a few inches from him on the bench.

"So I bumped into two ladies in the parking garage," Cowboy Hat said with a laugh as George's ears perked up.

Polka Dot nodded a reply and Cowboy Hat continued:

"They couldn't find their car. Can you believe that? I mean, how do you lose a car?"

George reached down and pretended to tie a shoelace, altogether stunned by what he was hearing.

"I'm not following," Polka Dot said shaking her head. "What did they want from you?"

Cowboy Hat smiled. "They wanted me to help them find their car. They couldn't remember where they parked it."

Polka Dot nodded and then glanced over at George, who instantly looked away. "So, did you help them?" she asked.

"Well, at first I told them I couldn't on account of having to pick up Gladice," Cowboy Hat said as he adjusted his earpiece. "But then one of them said they'd been looking for hours."

Polka Dot bit her bottom lip as though she was in pain, "Hours?"

Cowboy Hat nodded, "Said she'd even gone ahead and called her "'good-for-nothing son,' but as usual, he was taking his sweet time."

George expelled an abrupt gasp and as both parties turned in his direction, he pretended to be the victim of an impromptu coughing fit, and they quickly looked away.

"So, did you help them?" Polka Dot asked again, tugging at her espadrilles once more.

Cowboy Hat smiled widely, "I did! Found it in all of two minutes," he said excitedly.

George's mouth slack-jawed open as he digested this particular piece of information. He was tempted to interrupt, but decided to let it play out.

"Two minutes? Come on!" he heard Polka Dot say.

Cowboy Hat slapped his knee for emphasis: "All I did was push the panic button on the keychain. Their car was just a couple rows over."

"Bravo!" Polka Dot exclaimed and punched Cowboy Hat playfully on the shoulder. "You did a good deed!"

Cowboy Hat nodded, but then his face struck a serious conjecture. "The funny thing is I feel bad for the son."

"Whatdaya mean?" Polka Dot said, putting a stick of sugarless gum in her mouth.

"Well, I offered to track the guy down," Cowboy Hat explained. "You know, so he would know that they found the car and he wouldn't have to stick around."

Polka squinted her eyes, "So why didn't you?"

"They wouldn't give me a physical description," Cowboy Hat said as he shook his head. "They flat out refused."

Polka Dot crossed and then uncrossed her legs, "Refused?"

"Yeah, they just grabbed their suitcases and said '"The hell with him. That it served him right.'"

George dropped his head, closed his eyes and began rubbing at his temples. Inside his chest, in the approximate location of his heart, he felt a pang of discomfort—almost as though a wound he'd sustained years ago had unceremoniously reopened. When he at last rose to his feet, he glanced at Polka Dot, wondering if she, like all the women in his life, would cause him nothing but pure, unadulterated heartache.

The scene shifts now to the adjacent airport parking lot. Specifically, Lot 4, Row B:

Through the window of the late-model car, George gazed at the sky and as he studied the expanse—at the very grandeur before him, he could not help but gulp at his own smallness. Inchoate thoughts of God and the universe seared through his brain, raced across nerve endings and finally dissolved on some long-since-functional synapse. Just another late-model child in the deep, hot night.

George's thoughts drifted to Polka Dot, who now strolled across the lot, like an eidolon she flounced over the pavement, a large, oversized Gladstone in tow. As he watched with maxium interest, George couldn't quite fathom that she was alone, trailed by no one. Scratching his head, his mind churned out any number of scenarios that might have explained this. Some were wild. Some were humdrum. But none were correct. And now, as Polka Dot shilly-shallied, she looked back in his direction, that omniscient radar of hers perked up: he'd been detected.

As she approached, George fumbled with the radio, hoping to throw her off. He was generally a sucker for heart-wrenching ballads (most of which were beyond his vocal range), but tonight, as though in honor of Polka 'Dot's presence, a show tune began to play. He thought it was from *South Pacific* or maybe *Guys and Dolls*, but damn if it was not catchy.

The conversation was at first cold and unloved, like an unused pitcher of water:

"Say, do you happen to know anything about taxis?"

"What's that?" George asked as he pretended to fumble with the radio dial.

"Taxis," Polka Dot repeated leaning her head ever so slightly inside the car's window. "Do you happen to know where I could get one?"

George looked up from the radio and blinked, trying his best ignore the girl's beauty. "Um," he said casually as he searched into the distance, "I think they line up just outside of the main gate."

"Thanks. Thanks a lot." Polka said as she turned at the waist back toward the airport.

"No problem," George said, looking at the girl in the eyes for the first time. "None at all, actually. My pleasure."

Polka Dot nodded, but lingered, jingling her house keys. George shoegazed. She could have easily been on her way he thought, *easily*. But something crescendoed in the silence, in their short nervous breath, as though they were awkward young lovers. Then, without pretext, Polka 'Dot's eyes widened as she spotted the mountain of tennis balls piled high in the backseat.

Soon they were discussing grip sizes and string tensions and how they hated it when people left the lids of their cans behind and how it always made each of them a bit sad to pass by an empty, unused tennis court. He mentioned that he played a lot. She mentioned that she'd love to get back into it. And then without warning, without his usual diffidence, George made his play:

"If you wanted to hit sometime, let me know."

Polka Dot blinked her eyes her not once, not twice, but three times. "Sure!" she said with a trifle too much enthusiasm. "I'd love to!"

And before George knew it, they had made plans. Plans! And right then, and right there, he decided that all was forgiven—that he would send the Madwoman a dozen roses and maybe even show up for Sunday dinner.

As George stared happily at Polka Dot, very nearly gushing, it dawned on him that the girl before him remained nameless and that a descriptor like Polka Dot would no longer do. But he was almost afraid to spoil it—as though the exchange of such information would somehow sabotage the moment. Before he had the chance to inquire, he was no longer alone in the car, and the creature sitting next to him, as though having read his mind, was whispering that very thing into his ear. It was a pleasant name, one he cannot bring himself to say aloud, yet was quickly inscribed on that mental scrapbook of his—for now, she had her very own page:

"You know, it suits you."

"What's that?"

"Your name. It suits you."

"Thanks. It was my grandmother's."

"What's that?"

"My name. My name was my grandmother's."

"Oh."

"Listen, are you in a terrible hurry?" Polka Dot asked, glancing at the dashboard clock. "Not so much. Not *now*."

"I saw you at the gate," Polka Dot said. "Were you supposed to pick somebody up? I mean, not that it's any of my bus-"

"My mother. I was *supposed* to pick up my mother." George scratched at his face and cleared his throat, "It's kind of a long story. Let's just say she managed to find her own way home."

"Oh, well that's good."

"How about you?" George asked, turning down the radio volume.

"Me? I just had to pick up my bag. My Gladstone," the girl said, patting the leathered item on her lap. "The airline lost it. They offered to deliver it. You know, if I didn't want to drive all the way out? But I had to return the car."

George raised an eyebrow, "Return the car?"

"Yeah, it was a rental," Polka Dot said breathlessly. "*They're* coming out with a car for me next weekend. You know, the Fourth of July?"

George smoothed out the collar of his shirt and tried to remain casual, "They?"

"Mommy and Daddy," Polka Dot said matter-of-factly.

"I see . . . well, that'll be good," George said doing his best to hold up his end of the conversation. "Having a car and all, I mean."

Polka Dot glanced out the window. "Yeah," she said slowly, "it's been hard on them."

George again raised an eyebrow, "Hard?"

Polka 'Dot's head swiveled back toward George, "Me moving away and all."

"Oh, well yeah. That *can* be tough." George said, hoping to not come off as too much of a stiff.

"They wanted to buy me a pet," Polka Dot went on, "a bunny or something."

George set his right elbow on the middle armrest. "You mean bunny as in a rabbit?"

"Yeah," Polka Dot nodded. "They thought I'd be lonely in my apartment. So they wanted to buy me one. I used to have one when I was a kid. I'm not supposed to have pets though. I told them I couldn't. I felt sorta bad. . ."

George cleared his throat, "Well, it was a nice gesture, but I'm sure they understand. I mean if your building won't allow it, there's not much you can-"

"Say, do you live around here?" Polka Dot interrupted. "I mean the reason I ask"-"

"I go to university," George replied. "I'm home for the summer."

Polka Dot stared at George a second. "Oh. Well, I was just looking for a decent laundromat. My building has them, the machines I mean, but they're always occupied . . . "

George watched the girl play with the ends of her hair. "There's actually one near the park"," he said. "You know, where the courts are? I could probably"-"

"Swell," Polka Dot said with a smile. "I mean if you wouldn't mind pointing it out and all."

"Sure," George said good-naturedly. "No problem. I'd be happy"-"

Polka Dot abruptly turned around in the car and looked at the back seat. "Say, see all those balls of yours?"

"Yeah," George said, giving a cursory look over his shoulder.

"Well, my dad makes them."

George blinked his eyes, "Your dad makes tennis balls?"

"Uh uh," Polka Dot said with pride. "He has his *own* factory and everything. I have to be careful who I tell though. You'd be surprised how many people ask, you know, if they can have a case or two? The worst part is, most of them don't even play. They just want them for their dogs or kids or something."

"I can see how that could be a problem," George said mockingly. I'll tell you what, I'll consider that information *strictly* confidential. In fact, if you'd like, I mean, if you'd feel more comfortable I'll even sign a non-disclosure agreement."

Polka 'Dot's face broke out into a wide smile. "Funny. Very funny."

"Sorry," George said unable to control his laugh, "I couldn't' resist."

Polka Dot reached over and put a hand on George's shoulder, "It's okay," she said with an air of tenderness. "I don't *really* mind."

After several seconds of staring at one another, George broke his gaze and consulted his watch. "Hey, is there the slightest chance you'd want to eat?"

"I'm not especially hungry," Polka Dot said, placing a hand on her stomach, "but sure, I could eat."

Forgetting himself, George slid over in his seat, "Is there the slightest chance I could kiss you?"

"I'm not especially averse"-"

Through the window of the late-model car, *they* gazed at the sky and as they studied the expanse—at the very grandeur before them, they could not help but gulp at their own smallness. Inchoate thoughts of God and the universe seared through their brains, raced across nerve endings and finally dissolved on some long-since-functional synapse. Just another pair of late-model children in the deep, hot night.

CHAPTER 9: BEDTIME

George Martian raced through the frat house. The urgency on his face, the length of his stride, provides the barest of detail. He could have been late for class. Perhaps a date. But as it happened, it was 10:00 p.m. on Friday, the 10th of May, and that could only mean one thing: Springfest—a weeklong, decadent party leading up to graduation.

He had started getting ready at 9:00 and made great time—freshly showered, teeth brushed, hair gelled, contacts inserted, but got bogged down with the *other* thing: a singular misaligned thought, a weird mental kabuki that had plagued him ever since returning from Easter break.

As he stood before the bathroom mirror making some final and no doubt needless adjustments, he did his best to fight it off—to expunge the very memory of his and Mother's post-dinner conversation.

"Your sister left you a note, you know. Scrawled it out on the vanity mirror. Before she, well, offed herself."

He'd been standing in the center of the kitchen with a dishrag between his hands, the smell of Virginia-baked ham filling his boyhood home. He remembered doing a full-body double-take, of lunging toward his mother and slowly opening his mouth.

"That. That happened *years* ago," he'd said as his mind cartwheeled, "and you're just getting around to telling me now? *Now?*"

His mother had stepped her slippered feet backward,

looking surprised, perhaps a trifle hurt. "I didn't think you could handle it then," she'd countered.

"Handle it? Handle it? And what makes you think I can *now*?"

Presently, George directed a long and oddly ponderous look at his reflection. For the last several minutes he'd been fixated on the lower-right corner of the bathroom mirror, where a lone patch of shower-fog remained. Blinking his eyes in a slow, rhythmic manner, his expression was along the lines of someone working up to something, of trying to muster requisite nerve. Suddenly, he raised his left hand and employing his index finger, he scrawled out his sister's missive verbatim:

Georgie—it's ALL your fault. Daddy and me checking out. EVERY last bit of it. You're aces kiddo! Aces!

As George stared at his late sister's words, he could keep himself together no longer, and in that instant, in that one long headfucking moment, his mind teetered and then, all at once, dislodged itself: a strange sensation from just underneath his forehead—his frontal lobe to be precise. It was as though someone had used tweezers to remove a splinter. Only, whatever was extracted was never intended to be disturbed. His reflection was suddenly unfamiliar and for a full minute, he was unaware of who or where he was.

Time after ungodly time he'd recounted their fateful, nighttime rendezvous, and here it was once more. There was a trueness to it. Countable years of deep-going, of second-guessing that always left him in an unremitting state. Maybe it was just the oddments of life—of being duped and beclouded by an older, far wiser sister. After all, he was, by that time, damaged—overmatched in wits and, seemingly, in all other ways that might have revealed her true intent. He'd found her in the tub in the late morning. He saw it now in his brain-cage, a cortical vision at an oddly maligned depth: splayed and bloodied, awash, in of all things, bubble bath. It was an adult-sized moment, far bigger than for a child like himself. The screaming and blatting. The onrush of Mother. The hellish, innumerable weeks of greensick. And now, after all these years, a little keepsake from the grave delivered by way of Mother, the vessel: untold blame, unyielding guilt. The unwhisperable subject. If only there were some escape, a distant, but redeeming sacrament. But no.

As George rocked violently back and forth on the bathroom floor, he experienced a heightened sense of the present and swore he could feel one half of his brain dislodge from the other—not unlike the shifting of tectonic plates. Instinctively, he attempted to set things right by pressing his palms hard against his skull and hanging on for dear life.

"Georgie? Georgie boy, you okay in there?" came a baritone from the opposite side of the bathroom door.

As George lay in a pool of what he assumed was sweat, he just managed to gather himself. "Fine, Kurt," he grunted. "Fine."

"You're making some awful noises," Kurt Muldoon said. "And not to alarm you, but, as your housemate for the last four years, I feel compelled to inform you that there's, well, urine coming out from under the door."

There was a brief pause in the conversation as George attempted to circumvent the urine that was soaking through his freshly laundered shirt. "Must be a leak," he said with mounting panic. He cleared his throat and sat up prone on his left elbow. "I'll-I'll-I'll give maintenance a call."

Kurt Muldoon expelled a buoyant, collegial laugh, the kind that was prevalent among persons of his type of youth. "Dude, you had *another* Garbage Plate, didn't you? Serves you right! They give you the Runs man. The Runs!"

George waited for his housemate's laugh to subside and figured it best to play along, "Yeah, Garbage Plate," he said as he attempted, but failed, to sit up straight.

"Extra hot sauce?" Kurt asked with amusement.

"Yep," George managed to say.

"You gonna be able to rage tonight man? Gonna be an epic, epic night," Kurt said with a bit of a nasally laugh attached to the last syllable.

"I-," George gulped as a wave of impending doom engulfed him. "I don't know."

"Dude, you sound funny. Sure you're okay?" Kurt Muldoon asked as he jiggled the door handle. "Your voice is all freaky."

George bridged his hand over his eyes and cleared his throat. There's was just no way he could admit he was in midst of falling apart. "I'm *fine*," he said, doing his best to sound natural. "That Garbage Plate is just *really* wreaking havoc."

Kurt Muldoon sighed heavily through the door, "Alright man," he said, "feel better." He then banged a knuckle on the door and said, "Got a keg to tap!" and he was gone.

Several throbbing minutes later, George rose to his feet and headed toward his bedroom. Sleep will be the escape, he thought. In the morning all will be right. He managed to flop into the top bunk, but after a solid hour was unable to settle down. The problem lay with him, not the bed: for every time he closed his eyes he saw his sister's missive, each unwavering word, each letter floating, almost ghostlike through the engine room of his mind.

As the hours passed, he tossed and turned. The panic mounting with each tick of the clock. At various times, he heard his housemates enter and within minutes noted they were steadily dozing. He opened his eyes and squinted as he struggled to look through the tangle of bunks and bodies. He decided he could no longer lie still and sat up, his legs hanging over the bunk. He climbed down uncertainly in the darkness, afraid of alerting the man below, let alone the others. He tiptoed through the doorway and into the bathroom, seemingly the only place for a proper breakdown. Here, George paced, desperately trying to make sense of things, desperately trying to cleave to the remaining logic, an ordered sequence of thought that might pinpoint the glitch, the underlying factor. As he studied his face in the mirror, he told himself that it was going to be alright. That whatever was happening was normal, a mere formality in the grand scheme of things. Before returning to bed, though, he medicated: the remains of a warm, errant beer. As he stumbled back through the darkness, he noticed other bottles, and in quick succession, guzzled them. By the time he climbed under the blankets, he was decidedly buzzed. He rolled to his side and was nearly asleep, but his eyes passed over the clock: 3:43 a.m. Abruptly, his eyes widened and the panic surged and whatever favorable effect the booze extolled was gone.

By morning, he'd learned to the true meaning of time: of hours, of minutes, of seconds. He consumed a small warehouse of food at brunch, horrifyingly unaware that the fork recurrently missed its mark.

"Hey! Georgie boy!" a hungover Bob Pratt said from across the breakfast table. "Where the hell were you last night? It was epic man. Epic!"

George looked up from his waffle and blinked. He would've liked to disclose that he was in the midst of losing his mind, that the belated missive from his sister had triggered a balls-out mental collapse, but among *this* crowd, he was too much of coward to reveal such information.

"Under," George mumbled. "Under the weather," he said and kept on eating.

Kurt Muldoon, who had just sat down opposite George, gave his housemate a quick once-over. "Tell the truth, George," he said playfully. He then shifted in his chair and, with a full grin, addressed the table: "Old Georgie here had one too many Garbage Plates. Spent the night on the can!"

There was collective laugh from the table, and as George tensed up, he did his best to laugh along with them. These were his friends, he thought, his brothers, and there was just no way he could let whatever was happening to him jeopardize that.

George wandered aimlessly about the campus for the day. As he chanced upon the campus gazebo he stopped to reminisce. The mere sight of it evoked late-night encounters with girls. Blonde and brunette. Planned and unplanned. Drunk and sober. This had been the height of his powers, he thought, and as he grabbed his crotch he realized with horror that sleep wasn't the only thing he was no longer capable of.

Just then, a girl in a butterscotch plaid mini skirt and a roll neck sweater tapped him on the shoulder. "Hey,

George! Psyched about tonight?"

George wakened with a start—a jolt really, and stared back at the nameless girl with objective wonder. His memory of her was purely fragmentary: eyes, freckles, lips—but any more than that, and his rather tattered mind would've overshot the mark.

"It's Charlotte, George," the girl said inching forward. "Charlotte."

George forced a smile and expelled a slight grunt. He could feel himself tense up as a hot flush came over his face. "Hey, Charlotte."

"You're sweating like a madman, George," the girl said squinting her eyes. "You okay?"

A second later, George waved the girl off. "Flu. Fever," he said. "You want no part of this," and stormed off.

On the second night, George would lie in bed by the hour, fighting himself. Opening and closing his eyes. Fretting over when he'd sleep. Fretting over how he'd ever manage the upcoming trip abroad. There were times he was nearly out, only to be jarred to life by a falling sensation—distinct and clear, yet a bodily movement known only to him. At dawn, he rose and went for a run, with the dim hope that this, or some other method of exhaustion, would finally put him out.

That afternoon, George hid out in the library, wandering aimlessly from shelf to shelf, eventually stumbling upon the self-help section. He checked that no one was looking before sifting through a handful of titles:

The Harvard Medical School Guide to a Good Night's Sleep

The Promise of Sleep
Fall Asleep Easily
Healthy Sleep Habits, Healthy Child
*The No-Cry Sleep Solution for Toddlers and
    Preschoolers*

Among the facts discerned was the passing mention that the smell of old books had, in some instances, been known to induce sleep. With that, he was off: the rare book room. There in the half-light, he settled in. He lay recumbent in a seldom-used leather chair, taking in deep breaths of what pleasantly reminded him of fresh-cut wood. Some forty minutes later, the first editions proved no more obliging than his dorm room paperbacks. He left in despair, drifting aimlessly.

On the third night, George camped out in the frat house attic on a makeshift cot. The notion of trying to sleep with the others was far too much. The room itself had been designated as a sort of boy–girl rendezvous point, a frat house sex-spot for impromptu pre-, mid-, and post-party hook-ups. As George lay in a lordotic posture, he stared at the ceiling, listening to the din of partygoers on the floors below: the small talk, the big talk, the beer-soaked laughter. He recognized voices and, at times, swore he could even hear his own. As he sat up in bed, he reached over and downed another swig of Benadryl, knowing full well it would have no effect. Scratching his face, he was slowly, regrettably coming to the realization he was sorely in need of help. As the night bled into day, he tossed and turned, all the while paralyzed by a trembling melody of fear—fear of not being able to sleep, fear of being discovered, fear that he was going to be indentured to a lifetime's worth of madness.

When the early-morning sun shone through the window George tiptoed to the shower. He hadn't bathed in days and thought it best to at least try to give the appearance of normal. As he came around the corner he ran smack into a towel-only junior, Tad Gant.

"Jesus, George, haven't seen you in days," he said with a smile. "Who you got holed up in there with you, anyway?" he asked gesticulating toward the attic.

George ran a hand through his dirty hair and clenched his jaw. He could feel himself mentally untethering by the second.

"Just. Just some girl."

Tad Gant smacked George on the shoulder and issued a congratulatory wink. "It's that freshman I saw you with last week, isn't' it? Come on, out with it!"

George stepped backward and leaned up against the wall. "She's a wildcat, Tad," he said without any emotion. "An absolute wildcat."

"Good for you, dog! Good for you!" Tad Gant said and then shuffled past George down the hall.

By the fourth night, George was uncertain as to what was happening. In truth, the only thing he was entirely sure of was that he'd been wide awake. The bed was now an instrument of torture, and as he climbed in, he was like a hostage returning to his captor. Several misbegotten hours later, he escaped. He spent the remainder of the night creeping about the frat house, marveling at how the others were able to sleep. As he moved from slumbering body to slumbering body, it was as though they were circus performers, executing impossible trick upon trick.

By the fifth night, the panic and exhaustion were immeasurable. Unruly happenings surged through George's innerworkings and he did not like the way the room was looking at him. When morning broke, George had reached a sort of mental impasse—a realization that he was going to have to dial in some help.

Mother arrived at light speed, and to the emergency room they went. Under a watty glare of lights, doctors asked him his name and what day it was and other silly questions that he was unable to answer. Test results were inconclusive. They used vague terms like chemical imbalance. . . increased production of toxic neurochemicals . . . an undersupply of amino acids.

George sat on the edge of the examining table surrounded by white coats. He'd been poked and prodded for the last two hours and wasn't sure how much more he could take. "Can't you just put me on a drip-feed?" he begged. "I just want to be induced into an intravenous stupor. Indefinitely."

The white coats stared back, marked their charts, but said nothing. From a distant room, George could hear his mother clearing her throat.

"You can even perform experiments," George said desperately. "I don't care. Anything to avoid the tossing and turning. Anything. Just, please. Please put me out."

That night, George convalesced with his mother at a nearby hotel. He could see the campus from the fifth-floor window and, as a fresh wave of panic surged, he had to look away. "I can't let them know about any of this," he said. "Once I'm labeled a crazy, they'll be done with me. Done!"

"You're going to be fine, George. Just fine," his mother

said as she wrapped an arm around him.

George plunked down on the edge of his bed and buried his face in his palms. He was exhausted from head to foot—all parts of his mind, body, and soul seemingly at the tipping point.

"You NEVER should've told me about Annabelle's lovely little kiss-off," he said. "You shoulda just left me with the Goddamn illusion that everything was fine."

His mother sat down next to him and crossed her legs at her ankles. "I *thought* you'd be able to handle it," she said after a perceptible hesitation. "I thought it was time you knew."

George sat up straight and took a deep breath without any sense of relief. He was so tired, he thought he had a fever.

"Everything *was* fine," he said rubbing his somnolent eyes. "Perfect, actually. "And now, thanks to you, I can't sleep. For five *whole* days. Five! And I'm, I'm . . . an absolute basket case."

His mother stared at him like a therapist-in-training coming to terms with all the facts. "I feel positively terrible about it, George. Just terrible," she said taking hold of his hand. "You're *absolutely* right," she went on, "I *never* should've told you. Never."

George turned to his mother and blinked his eyes just once: "You're damn right!"

His mother grasped his hand tight, and then for emphasis, shook it, "But *now* I'm here to help," she said as tears streamed down her face. "Now I'm here to make sure you get better."

George tilted his head to the floor and stared dejectedly into space. There was an element of hopelessness in the room, he thought, of unobjectionable tragedy and unsure of what else to do, he issued a protracted snort: "And how exactly are you going to do that?"

On a sudden but pressing impulse, Mrs. Martian abruptly grabbed her purse. "Do you know how many different kinds pills they gave you?" she said as she began setting out bottle after bottle on the bedstand.

George watched his mother with mild interest, but made no reply.

"Seven, George!" Seven. An absolute army!" Mrs. Martian said. "You're going to sleep, George," she said taking his head between her hands. "You're going to sleep!"

George watched his mother pull back the sheets and then he climbed under. A moment later, she gave him a glass of water and fed him a cocktail of pills—red, blue, and orange; round, oblong, diamond-shaped.

"I don't think I can do it," he said as he lay back on the pillow and squirmed. I don't think I'm going to sle-"

"The pills are going to work, George"," his mother said firmly as she crouched over him. "But you have to let them. You have to surrender. Understand?"

George closed his eyes and took a full-capacity breath. In the background, he heard the ceiling fan turn on. As his mother massaged his back, she whispered, "Sooner or later you'll fall asleep. Let yourself go. Think happy thoughts."

"It's not going to work," George said a moment later as he sat up in bed and looked wide-eyed at his mother.

Mrs. Martian frowned in the darkness, "My goodness George, you haven't even been in bed for five minutes. You've got to give it some time. Now lay lie down."

For the next several minutes George tossed and turned. The impossibility of sleep was overwhelming. He kept hearing his mother whisper, "Sooner or later you'll fall asleep. Let yourself go. Think happy thoughts," to the point that it, like the fan, became part of the acoustics of the room.

Twenty minutes later, George could feel something happen in the undercurrents of mind, tiny tremors of release as the army of pills took hold.

Sooner or later you'll fall asleep. Let yourself go. Think happy thoughts.

He fought off the urge to again check the clock and managed to sit still for the next several minutes. Something was happening, he thought, and before he knew it, he felt not unlike a stick of warm butter melting away in a frying pan.

Sooner or later you'll fall asleep. Let yourself go. Think happy thoughts.

As he lay on his back, he became conscious of his mother pulling the comforter to a point just under his nose. He remembered her doing the same thing every night of his childhood as she'd tucked him in, and while he could never say why exactly, he'd always liked it.

Sooner or later you'll fall asleep. Let yourself go. Think happy thoughts.

The fan was nice, he thought. So was the blanket. But the lilt of his mother's voice was the cat's meow. Suddenly, for no particular reason, George pictured a rocket on the verge of taking off. He could feel his mind, hell his whole body, rumble on the launch pad, and as it broke ground, George could feel himself blast off, an oblivion he'd never thought he'd see again.

When George awoke the next morning, he remained unconvinced he'd slept. He demanded proof. Evidence.

When his mother asked him how he felt, he surprised himself by saying, "Better."

They repeated the ritual night in and night out. With each subsequent victory, George regained a bit of his former self, though not entirely. After a full week, his mother headed home.

"Damn, George!" Where you been?" Kurt Muldoon said as George pulled into the frat house driveway and applied what was, at best, questionable brakes. George turned off the ignition, stepped out of the car, and watched his housemate light up a joint. "Had a funeral back home," he said with all the sincerity he could muster. "Kind of unexpected. A last-minute thing."

Kurt Muldoon closed his lighter and fingered it back into the pocket of his jeans. "Sorry, man. My condolen-"

"Don't worry about it," George said relieved that his housemate was stoned. "Just a distant relative."

Kurt Muldoon nodded and inhaled a single drag of smoke. "Well, good to have you back," he said cheerfully and punched George on the shoulder. "Seems like forever."

George reached into the car and grabbed his duffle bag. "Yeah, I know," he said sheepishly. "Good to *be* back." George cleared his throat, "So what exactly did I miss?"

Kurt Muldoon shook his head sideways a few times and then blew a faulty smoke ring skyward. "Nothing really. Just the normal shenanigans," he said, holding up the joint."

George forced a smile, but said nothing. He could feel his meds wearing off and wanted very badly to reach into his pocket for another pill.

"Hey," Kurt Muldoon said suddenly and punched

George in the shoulder once more. "I just remembered," he said exhaling another drag of smoke. "Our passports came! All of 'em!"

George stepped back as his face struck a serious conjecture. He'd completely forgotten about the trip abroad—the one he not only singlehandedly planned but campaigned for. As he stared back at his housemate he wanted very badly to just come out with it: to tell him he was under a doctor's care, that he now relied on a cocktail of pills to sleep and well, hell, to even get through the day; that he'd very nearly lost his mind and was now, only, just barely able to hold it together; and lastly that there was just no way he'd make the big trip.

George looked at his housemate with feigned excitement. "Good man! Good!" he said. "Should be an excellent, excellent trip," and without so much as waiting for a reply, quickly shuffled his way toward the house.

It was a wall-to-wall-carpet two-bedroom apartment, "a regular bachelor pad," his mother had announced cheerfully when she'd helped him move in. Seventeen and one-half miles from his boyhood home, and a mere three miles from Dr. Seabring's office. It was also, as luck would have it, an ideal spot from the elementary school gig he'd managed to nab, his classroom window actually bordering the parking lot of his apartment complex.

George moved about the room, neither panicked nor calm, making a series of final bedtime adjustments: the drapes, the alarm clock, the thermostat, the fan. The fan. How the very sound of it pleased him. How it lifted his spirits. How its counterfeit breeze tingled his flesh and, if only for a moment, released him. Then, with one deliberate motion, he pulled the blankets apart and slid under. Lying on his back, he stretched the sheet so that it sat just below the nose. He could not say why exactly, but the covering of his mouth afforded him additional comfort. And it did not end there, for George now reached and put his arm around his number one companion. They were cheek to cheek. It would romantic, if not for the fact that the creature next to him was a stuffed animal—a lamb he'd had since he was an infant. It was ragged and frayed by now, so much so that he kept it in a ziplock bag under the bed during daylight hours.

As George waited for the pills to take hold he recited his mantra: *Sooner or later you'll fall asleep. Let yourself go. Think happy thoughts.* He repeated it a half dozen times before indulging in his evening escapades. Just the sort that the good Dr. Seabring suggested. He pictured himself floating down the Mississippi on a raft, a la Huck Finn. As night falls, he lies down and drifts off into the rivered night. Next, he's sharing a train ride with his old university pals as they rumble off toward parts unknown. He pictures himself trading stories while a nameless girl in polka dots gives him a foot massage. When these failed to subdue him, his mind wandered to a new scene, one that is not yet Dr. Seabring-approved: he stands behind a pile of cardboard boxes in the Texas School Book Depository as he peers at one Mr. Lee Harvey Oswald. As the killer brings the rifle to his shoulder, he abruptly turns around and smirks at his witness.

George gasped for breath and lurched upward. As his heart raced, he dry-swallowed one of the many pills on his bedstand and went directly to the fan. As the air blew over him he repeated his mantra: *Sooner or later you'll fall asleep. Let yourself go. Think happy thoughts.* After some fifteen repetitions, George stumbled back to bed. He did not permit himself to consult the alarm clock. He sat on the edge of the bed. Slumped, he was conscious of posture, the obscene angles at which his bones hung, and at the moment, even this aspect of himself he hated.

As George fell further into brown study, he was abruptly stirred to the present by way of his cat's claws. Pluto. The fickle bitch had been Dr. Seabring's idea, when he'd first taken the apartment. Just as she burrowed into his lap, though, George rose. He consulted the alarm clock and quickly tabulated the remaining hours till work. He stood over the bedside table and although he had already achieved the *recommended dosage,* he swallowed another pill, an orange one. George then began to thumb through a leather-bound journal that sat next to his bed. It had been a gift from Mother, for the trip abroad. His plan had been to document his and his friends' travels—the grand times they were having—to record every moment of their wild, decadent romp. Instead, like his seat on that transatlantic flight, the pages of the journal remained empty. He'd spent nearly a year planning it, nearly a year convincing all twelve of them they must come along. That this, their Cook's tour of Europe, would be the trip to end all trips— the culmination of their four years together, one last triumphant march through their very own brand of juvenilia. As the tears fell, George eyed the many unpacked boxes that littered the room, among them, a shoebox— postcards his friends all sent of the grand time *they* were having: gondola rides, ferryboats, train stations—them: the boys and girls of America, and him: not now, not ever, a part of it.

When the orange pill did not overtake his consciousness, George knew he would have to resort to his fail-safe. The one method that would do the proverbial trick. And so, at 2:42 a.m., he dialed the number. Though it had been months since he last resorted to such measures, it was scarcely a full ring when the voice picked up. The conversation was brief, but nonetheless calm, and most importantly, reassuring. Seconds later, as he drifted off, there was a smile on his face. Mother had saved him. Again. Had there been time for his prayers, he would have prayed that she outlived him. It was all he ever prayed for.

CHAPTER 10: HONEYMOON

He wondered, with erection in hand, how exactly to negotiate the mystery between his young bride's legs. For although George was familiar with such regions, Ginnie had insisted that all lights in 507, the *honeymoon suite,* be put out. George plunged in full bore, though, hoping for the best. Ginnie expelled a few gasps, and, thinking he'd found the right locale, he intensified his thrusts. It was not until she started to cough and pat him, not so lovingly on the head, that he realized he was attempting to penetrate his young bride's belly button (an "inny" as a matter of fact). She issued a giggle and redirected, whispering that he "need not worry," that she was still "as wet as a waterfall."

The hotel concierge, a Mr. Glass, had assured him that everything had been arranged. That when they checked in, suite 507, a junior suite, would be referred to as a *honeymoon suite.* The rate, outside of a larger tip, would be the same. In fact, Glass had claimed that the rooms had identical dimensions—the sole distinction being that a junior suite consisted of two beds as opposed to one, and for a certain hotel guest, who, for lack of a better descriptor, suffered from some rather severe sleep issues, that made all the difference.

It had been Mother's idea. A good one at that. After all, for someone riddled with his affliction, and who was, by nature, habitually concerned with all things sleeping, a spare bed was a kind of lifeboat—a place in which to toss and turn freely, all without disturbing anyone who just so happened to be in proximity. In this case, Ginnie. Mother had even acquired some special pills, if things, as she liked to say, "got out of control." He had other pills of course— ones that had actually been prescribed to him—but these, these were special and would put him out in no time. How mother procured such pills she did not say, only that she "had a way with doctors." She'd encouraged him to take one every night. Whether he "needed it or not." "Just, you know, to be safe." Complicating matters was Ginnie's pre-wedding assertion that he stop any and all medication. That relying on such things could only lead to something unpleasant. Even tragic. That there were two camps, the pro-pill and the anti-pill, and she, having grown up in the latter, had never taken so much as an aspirin, and was all the better for it. He remembered looking her in the eye and nodding in agreement, all the while knowing full well that he'd disappoint. After all, in the seven years since the trouble began, he'd *always* needed something to help him sleep. And so, after an extended cuddling session, complete with pillow talk, George slipped out of bed, downed one of Mother's pills and again, hoping for the best, slipped into the adjacent twin bed. Oblivious to the whereabouts of her husband was the now deflowered bride, who was at present, fitfully dozing.

The room was dark, but not so dark as to prevent George from noticing the artificial forget-me-nots that littered the floor. He remembered there being a discussion. A controversy of sorts. Something about the good-for-nothing florist. How the bride had wanted, no, specifically requested, that the forget-me-nots be of the real-deal variety. How she didn't give a good goddamn how many people were waiting. She wasn't going down the aisle with *anything* artificial in her hair. Yet, an hour-plus later, after the urging of any number of people, including the priest, she'd done just that. As George turned to admire Ginnie, now in a noticeably calmer state, he started to feel a bit funny. There was a distinct tingling sensation emanating from parts unknown. At length, he felt like butter in a frying pan. Only instead of heat, there was a melting sensation. A boiling away. And then without warning, he was out. Discovering an oblivion he'd never known.

When morning came George felt drowsy and was conscious of a pain at the base of his neck. He surreptitiously made his bed and then slipped in next to his wife. He lay there for a good hour, studying the utter strangeness of his wedding band. He'd intended to remove it, as he preferred to sleep unfettered, but the potency of Mother's pills had not permitted such action. There was a relief in knowing he'd slept. That Mother's pills had worked. Now it was only a question of how to break the news. After all, he couldn't hide it forever.

By late morning Ginnie awoke. He had his mind set on the buffet, but after hearing Ginnie expound on the merits of scones and crepes, *they* settled on the Tea Room.

As per their special arrangement, Mr. Glass would handle all communications with Mother. Personally. That when and if she called, he would see to it that Mr. Martian, in 507, received the communication with the utmost speed and delicacy. That circumstance made it necessary that the young bride, Mrs. Martian, be kept in the dark. That it was positively crucial, CRUCIAL, that she not be made aware of any such communications. It was with this end in mind that Mr. Glass approached the Martians in the Tea Room:

"Ah, the Martians!" Glass said as he brushed a rather

troubling, but imaginary, piece of lint from the shoulder of his gabardine suit. "I trust everything is to your liking? That everything, as you American's say, is up to par? Yes?"

George looked up from the grapefruit on his plate and smiled. "Indeed," he said. "Everything is"-"

"About the room, Mr.?" Ginnie interrupted.

"Glass, my dear. The name is Glass," the concierge said inching a few steps forward. "You were saying?"

Ginnie glanced over at George and then turned back to Glass. "We have two," she said. "Two beds. It's just that it's *supposed* to be a honeymoon suite. It just seems odd is all . . ."

George reached out and put a delicate hand on Ginnie's forearm. This was exactly the kind of remark he'd been afraid of. "Babycakes, he said, "give the man a break." Then, turning to Glass, he replied, "Everything is top shelf Glass. Top shelf. You and your staff have really outdone yourselves."

Glass flashed a nervous smile and then said in his best the-customer-is-always-right tone, "Well, that's good to hear, sir. We here at the Frontenac pride ourselves on such matters."

"By the by, Mr. Martian," Glass went on, "I've made those snorkeling reservations you'd requested. I'll just need you to sign off on the pape"-"

"Oh George"!" Ginnie said, "clasping his hand. "You remembered!"

George smiled broadly, but before he could respond, Ginnie had turned to Glass.

I've always wanted to try it you know!" she said excitedly. "It just seemed, oh, I don't know, fun!"

"Splendid, Mrs. Martian. Just splendid"," Glass said

cheerfully. "Now, Mr. Martian, if you could just step this way and I'll direct you to those papers . . ."

On the sub-main floor of the Hotel Frontenac, on the south shore of St. Thomas, George reads over a correspondence he's just now been handed. He awkwardly holds a lighted Cuban in his right hand (compliments of Glass) and the missive in the other. He stops reading periodically to rub the back of his neck, which for some reason or other, is pulsating.

Georgie-

Well, you're married. Yes married. I just hope you've thought this through is all. She's pretty enough. Just a tad, well, temperamental. But after what happened at the church I guess you already know.

That Mr. Glass I spoke to seems like a very nice man. Be sure to tip him. He mentioned that the hospital is just two miles away. You know, just in case. Anyway, I put the pills in your suitcase when I packed it. They're right under your swim trunks.

I remain very concerned about you, Georgie. Very. I'm not altogether convinced this wife of yours is equipped to handle things. After all, this is your first big trip outside of my care. If only you'd 'mooned stateside. Where I could be closer. Nonetheless, I'll try not to worry, so long as you keep me apprised of things. Otherwise, I may go mad.

Love,
You know who

While Mother could be overbearing and intrusive, the

cardinal fact remained that it was George who'd involved her. It had been Saturday—exactly one week prior to the nuptials—that he'd confided. He was having doubts. Reservations. He hadn't wished to alarm her, of course. At least not unnecessarily. But, well, what if he couldn't sleep? On his honeymoon no less. He'd been a bachelor far too long, and now here, on the precipice of marriage, he could not bear the thought of spoiling things. She produced the pills the very next day. He remembered how she'd held the bottle out before him. Then just as she'd been about to hand them over, she flashed her all-but-canonized grin and pulled them back. The pills would come with a stipulation: that for the duration of the honeymoon he would have to remain in contact. That for the sake of *his* well-being he must—MUST—keep her apprised of his given mood. His state. And like all the trade-offs and half-deals that came before, he'd consented. Still, as he held the fountain pen above the hotel stationary, he couldn't quite bring himself to reply. And with that, George was snorkel-bound, knowing full well there'd be ramifications.

The shirtless groom in 507 was splayed out on the bed stomach side down while his young bride both dutifully and begrudgingly massaged his neck. The kink, *thought* to be aggravated by the snorkeling, had gotten worse.

"Any better?" Ginnie asked.

George grimaced. "No," he said with an air of injustice in his voice. "It hurt a little this morning, but I think the snorkeling did me in."

Ginnie sat back on her knees and, in the manner of someone unaccustomed to giving back rubs, shook her hands out. "Can you *at least* sit up?" she asked with limited patience. "Maybe moving 'round will make it feel better."

George issued a groan and rolled over such that he now lay on his right shoulder, facing Ginnie. He could tell she was about to fall into one her pouting routines, but he had no choice but to be honest: "Babycakes, think I'm down for the count," he said. "Maybe we ought to just order room service."

Ginnie sat down on the opposite bed and frowned. "Did you sleep funny or something?" she asked caustically. "Because I just don't, I just don't understand."

George kicked the top sheet clear off his toes as though the coverlet was too much for his debilitated body. "Must've," he said. "Not sure what else it could be."

From across the room, Glass stood at the ready. He held a clipboard and pen between his hands and was, in fact, finalizing the room service order the Martians were inevitably about to place. Moments ago, he'd suggested (as diplomatically as possible), that their dinner reservations in the Grand Ballroom be put on hold—that considering Mr. Martian's condition, the wearing of a suit coat and tie might be difficult, if not altogether impossible.

"Shall I go ahead then and place your order?" Glass asked as he politely stepped forward, butler-style.

George glanced over at Ginnie and then without so much as waiting for a response took charge: "Yes, Glass. Please. Go right ahead."

"Very good, sir," Glass said as he scrawled out some final instructions in a Getty-Dubay-trained handwriting. "Shall I fetch you the doctor?"

George rested his head against the headboard and eyeballed Ginnie. She was doing something with her face— the same sort of look he'd seen at the church when the flower order had been fouled up.

"NO!" Ginnie said with more than a touch of asperity as she abruptly reached over and began propping up George's head (rather frantically) on a pillow. "*He* won't be needing *any* doctor. *'I'll* take care of him."

George looked over at Glass for a rescue, but all he got was a consolation sigh. Then without so much as a word, Glass turned on his heels and made his exit.

Following a meal of roasted duck and pan-sautéed sea bass, the Martians settled in for an early night. The bride, flush with romance, raced to the bathroom, locked the door, and proceeded to pull out a folio-sized hardcover from her carry-on bag. *The Sex Bible: An Illustrated Guide.* She fingered the pages, many of which she'd previously dog-eared, in the hope of finding something to accommodate George and his crazy neck business. He'd already dropped hints about going straight to bed, but she'd be damned if she'd let a stiff neck stand in the way of *her* sex. After all, this was their honeymoon. As she sifted through the pages, she became intrigued by something titled "Cowgirl" and proceeded to study its various diagrams with high interest. In her absence, the bridegroom managed to just reach his own carry-on. From it, he swallowed not one, but two of Mother's pills. When the bride returned, she wore a periwinkle number complete with garter belts. Not getting the approval from her husband she was expecting (his eyes were nearly closed) she does her own version of the cannonball and plunges onto the bed. Jolted, the groom finds himself being mauled and before he knows it, he has been engaged. Hours of one-way sex pass before the bride realizes that her husband is out cold.

At 9 a.m. the occupants of 507 are jarred to life by way of the phone. Brody Jenkins, the Frontenac's resident tennis pro, was on the line. He heard a groggy "hello" on the other end and then began to read from a lined 3 X 5 index card:

This is a courtesy call regarding your first round match in the Sweetheart Open. You will be playing (pause) Dr. Raymond Abernathy and his wife, Rose, of (pause) Westport, Connecticut. Your match will begin at (pause) 11 a.m. sharp on Court (pause) 5.

Jenkins flipped the card over and continued:

This is a single-elimination tournament. First-round matches will consist of a ten-game pro-set. Participants will be allowed a fifteen-minute warm-up and should bring their own towels. Water and a fresh can of balls will be supplied. A complimentary lunch buffet, served alfresco, will follow the completion of the first round.

After taking a deep breath, Jenkins mustered a cheerful, *"See you on the courts!"* and promptly hung up.

George, who'd picked up the phone (it was on his side of the bed), vaguely remembered Ginnie making a passing mention about the tournament. In fact, now that he thought about it, she'd done so with a fair amount of gusto. For his young bride had been engendered with a fierce competitive spirit. So much so, that despite his head now being locked in a painful, skyward position, he knew there'd be no backing out. After all, despite Ginnie's schoolgirlish figure, there was something undeniably intimidating about her. An air, if you will, that what she said goes.

"Babycakes," George said as though he was the bearer of especially bad news, "I don't think I'm up to playing."

"Nonsense, George," Ginnie said as she laced up a sneaker. "Absolute nonsense."

George attempted to sit up straight in bed, but was overcome by a jolt of neck pain. Whatever was happening to him, he thought, was seemingly getting worse.

"It isn't nonsense," George said as he tried to speak with authority. "Now *please*, be reasonable."

At the window, Ginnie changed her position such that her back was facing George. "If you think this neck business of yours is going to ruin *our* honeymoon, you've got another thing coming,"' she said folding her arms across her chest. "Now get dressed."

George stared back at his wife and gulped. He ached from the base of his neck down to his shoulder blades—any movement beyond resulted in an onrush of pain.

"Listen, Ginnie," George said, "the last thing I want to do is ruin our honeymoon, but whatever is wrong with me is getting progressively worse. I need a doctor. Understand? A doctor."

Ginnie abruptly turned around and smoothed out the tennis skirt she'd bought specially for the tournament. Her eyes had begun to water up and as George studied her face, a singular, emotive tear was making its way down her cheek. "This means a lot to me, George. A lot," she said as she wiped at her face. "The tournament is one of the reasons why I wanted to book this place. We fell in love on a tennis court, George. You proposed to me on one. Don't you remember? Don't you?"

George rubbed his neck, "Of course I remember Babycakes. Of course. But-"

"But nothing," Ginnie said as she approached the bed and offered George her arm. "Now do this for me, will you?"

George looked into Ginnie's sad eyes and then at her delicately outstretched hand. A second later, he came away with the impression he had but little choice. "Okay," he said, "I'll try," and a second later, Ginnie hook-armed him to a standing position.

While in transit to the courts Ginnie stopped mid-stride and grabbed George by the arm. As they'd walked along in silence, George could tell her mind had been working up to something, but he couldn't say exactly what.

"This match is of the all-out-must-win variety," Ginnie conveyed at a buoyant, excitable volume.

With his head angled upward, George could just make out the very top of Ginnie's pony-tailed head, "Huh?"

"I mean, if you think I'm going to lose to that first-rate bitch, Rose Abernathy, you're flat out crazy."

George stood quietly for a moment as his mind digested this particular piece of information. After a few breaths, he employed both hands and slowly forced his head downward a few minor, excruciating inches, "Who?'"

"Rose Abernathy," Ginnie repeated, gripping the handle of racket tightly. "She took the last good pair of goggles and fins on the snorkeling trip. "Right out of my hands as a matter of fact!"

George let go of his face and his head instantly shifted upward. "Is that what this is all about?" Goggles and fins?"

Just then, from a point beyond George's immediate vision, Glass appeared. As he charged along the narrow pathway that led to the tennis courts, beads of sweat coursed down his rather majestic forehead.

"A moment of your time, sir," Glass said.

George blinked his eyes as Glass slowly came into view. There was an urgency to his tone, a resonance really, that made his words not so much a request, but a directive.

"We've a match to play," Ginnie growled as she cast a hostile look in Glass' direction. "Can't this wait?"

Glass smiled nervously. "I'm afraid not, dear," Glass said. "We're having an issue with your credit card. Besides, it'll only take but a minute, dear," he said. "I promise."

George turned to Ginnie and made a sort of mea culpa of his face. "I'll meet you at the courts," he said. "It'll give you a chance to warm up."

Ginnie expelled a hot breath and once again consulted her wristwatch. "Fine!" she said with a high degree of exasperation. "But make it quick, George! Quick!"

From under the clandestine shade of a parasol, Glass pulled out a slip of paper. "I've a note from your mother, sir," he said. "I had to tell her about the neck businesses."

George looked at Glass and frowned. "Why would you go and do that?"

Glass bowed his ahead repentantly. "I had to, sir. A contractual obligation. As you know, she's paying for this whole endeavor."

George sighed deeply and gingerly turned in the direction of the courts. In the distance, he could see Ginnie performing a series of warm-up stretches. "My mother's all riled up now, isn't' she? Probably wants me to cut things short and head home."

"Not exactly," Glass said and held up to the missive. "She says the reason for your ailment is the pills she gave you."

George raised his eyebrows and then all at once cringed, "Give it."

Georgie-

I am gravely concerned about you. Gravely. Not to mention very, very hurt. How is it you expect me to help when you don't keep me apprized? Thank goodness for this Glass fellow. If not for him, I'd know nothing of this neck business. Anyway, I forgot to tell you about the pills. They have side effects. I was going to call Dr. Renshaw, but figured I could handle it. After all, a little neck soreness isn't' going to kill you.

I trust that you're sleeping well? That the pills are working? I can only assume so. Have you told that wife of yours about them? The pills I mean. You need to stand up to her. I mean it!

Now pay attention Georgie because this is important: whatever you do, promise me that you'll KEEP TAKING THEM! The last thing you need is another sleeping episode on top of this neck business. I expect to hear from you, Georgie. And soon. I mean it!

Love,
Mommy

P.S. I have instructed Glass to keep tabs on you. Should your condition worsen, I may be forced to do something drastic.

After a second read-through, George crumpled up the paper and handed it to Glass. "I can't believe she'd give me something with side effects!" he said as he rubbed his neck. "I mean what exactly am I supposed to do here? Keep taking them like she said or risk an insomnia free fall?"

Glass cleared his throat and stepped forward. "Perhaps I should fetch the doctor."

George shook his head. "No," he said. "I can't risk it. If Ginnie finds out about the pills, I'm a dead man. Dead." Rising to his feet, George headed for the courts.

"What about your mother?" Glass called after him. "Shouldn't you write her back?"

George stopped in his tracks and turned back to Glass. "The hell with her! What is she going to do, fly down here?"

Characters: Mr. and Mrs. Martian, Dr. Raymond and Rose Abernathy. Time: 11:07 a.m. Location: Hotel Frontenac, Court 5. Props: Wilson Pro Staff, Dunlop 200G, Puma Power Beam Pro, Yonnex RdiS Mid and one can of just-opened Wilson heavy-duty tennis balls.

The Abernathy's were in their mid-forties or thereabouts. A second marriage for her, a third for him, George surmised. They were dressed from head to foot in the latest tennis apparel, having just that morning paid a visit to the Frontenac's pro shop (various price tags and shirtings were piled high on a nearby bench): Rose was all pink, donning a visored hat that was paired with a matching one-piece bodysuit. It was of the spandex/polyester variety, and, as George eyed her critically, he mused that even the most unbiased of spectators would find it a goodly number of sizes too small for her.

The doctor, or "Doc," as he introduced himself, was dressed in white, his only indulgence being a makeshift pink headband (obviously tied by his wife) that just so happened to match Rose's attire.

Ginnie's scouting report on the Abernathy's (which she relayed to George while trying to dislodge his head from its vexing upwardness) revealed that Rose was the "weak link." While she had solid "groundies," she had a "natural aversion to net play." Additionally, Ginnie went on to say, with a rather extravagant grin, the woman was "plagued by a general stoutness," resulting in "limited mobility," and thus was something they should "take full advantage of." George looked at Ginnie and thought about reminding her of his own lack of mobility, but ultimately decided against it. Instead, he only grunted, permitting her to expound on the good doctor, who, she was now just saying, "was lights out" at the net but "prone to error on the baseline." Then adding, with an air of someone who'd once been runner-up in junior nationals, that "his chief mechanical flaw" was an "inability to keep his elbow in on his forehand," which by the way, she pointed out, "was a common error among 3.5 players masquerading as 4.0 players."

After a stop at the watercooler and some final instructions from Jenkins, Martian vs. Abernathy was nearly underway. Dr. Abernathy stood at the baseline bouncing a ball up and down. He was about to serve, but hesitated and approached the net.

"Excuse me, George is it? Are you alright? You look as though you're in no condition to play."

George stood on the opposite side of the net with his head still locked in a decidedly skyward position. This was it, he thought. This was just the out he was looking for.

"Well, I am a little under the-"

"He'll be fine," Ginnie interjected in a noticeably strained tone of voice. "Just a little stiff neck is all."

The good doctor took a step forward and squinted his eyes as though he remained unconvinced. "Are you quite sure?"

George turned at the waist to face Ginnie, but all he could manage was guttural, losing protest.

"Serve the ball!" Ginnie said and the action commenced.

At forty minutes past eleven, or conversely, twenty minutes of twelve, all matches on surrounding courts had been decided. An assemblage of winners, losers, and Brody Jenkins watched in something close to amazement as a player by the name of Martian, who they mispronounced as Martin, made dazzling volley after dazzling volley. The feat was all the more of a spectacle due to Martian's highly unorthodox tennis form, which chiefly involved his rather obstinate fixation with looking skyward. There was a general chatter within the crowd about the merits of such form, triggering a rebuttal from Jenkins, who remarked to anyone within earshot that "relying solely on peripheral vision was outright dangerous." As Jenkins looked toward the court and watched Ginnie Martian double-fault, he pointed out that despite Martian's display, the match was now deadlocked at ten games apiece.

With the score tied, Jenkins met Team Abernathy and Martian at the net. As George sat down and deep-massaged his neck region, he only half-listened to Jenkins.

"This'll be a seven-point win-by-two tiebreak, folks. The winning team will, of course, advance to the much-coveted second round of the Sweetheart Open!"

It should be noted that various odors covering a wide array of gastronomy had begun to filter through the air. At length, spectators grow restless as lunchtime delights passed before their eyes and were in turn placed on nearby buffet tables.

The Martians took an early 3-1 lead in the tiebreak. Between points, George heard Ginnie court-whisper assorted instructions, but found himself no longer physically able to nod back. "Just a few more points," he said to himself. "Just a few more points." For the last several minutes he'd been overcome by a series of intermittent neck spasms. What was particularly unsettling was that the spasms appeared to be spreading to other regions—as though it was only a matter of time before they became something far worse. Unnerved, George issued back-to-back double faults on his serve, causing Ginnie to not only glare at him but expel a series of invectives.

On the ensuing changeover, the tiebreak was deadlocked at 3-3. With a wide smile on his face, Jenkins tried to lighten the mood by complimenting "the high level of play" to which neither team replied. Returning to court, the doctor unleashed a violent "kick" serve upon Ginnie, who was promptly aced. Leading 4-3, Abernathy then served to George: as the ball advanced toward him, the high bounce of the "kick" serve, allowed him to just make out the yellowed fuzz of the ball on his backhand side. With a grunt of pain, George lobbed the ball over Rose Abernathy, who stood ready at the net. As he watched her backpedal and align herself for an overhead slam, he gasped, but she swung wildly and missed the ball completely instead.

In the points that followed, the two teams remained

neck and neck. The crowd, due in large part to the luncheon, fell victim to attrition, leaving only Jenkins and a few diehards behind. At 6-6, Jenkins interrupted play to announce that whoever wins the next exchange will have match point. As though recognizing the stakes, a long rally ensued. George, standing at the net, survived a series of blistering forehands from Dr. Abernathy, but was unable to put any of them away. On the eleventh ball, Abernathy managed to sneak one past him, and while it appeared to just clip the line, Ginnie abruptly called it out. The remaining spectators responded with conspiratorial "oohs" and "ahhs" and, as though sensing they were missing something, many of the lunchers returned, plates in hand.

Dr. Abernathy: "Are you quite sure?"

Ginnie: "What's that?"

Rose: "The ball. He wants to know if it was *really* out. Because, well, it looked like it was *in*. You know, that it *caught the line*?"

Ginnie: "Oh."

Rose: "Well was it?"

Ginnie: ". . . ."

Rose: "Well?"

Before Ginnie could respond Jenkins intervened. While he had no real stake in the match, Frontenac Management had instructed him to, above all else, avoid controversy.

Jenkins: "Folks, in the interest of fair play, I think it best if we replay the point."

Ginnie: "But the ball was out."

Rose: "He *said*, replay it."

Ginnie: "But-"

Jenkins waves his hand dismissively and says, "REPLAY-THE-POINT." He then turns his back and with finality heads to the sidelines.

As George watched Ginnie expel a deep sigh, he did his best to avoid eye contact. A second later, she, begrudgingly, served. From opposite baselines, the women exchanged a series of forehands—the angles and pace were of such quality that the men were rendered spectators. The intensity escalated to the point that with each strike of the ball came a Monica Seles–type grunt. On the fifteenth ball, Ginnie grew impatient and rushed the net. Rose countered with a near-bullet return, forcing Ginnie to attempt a one-handed backhand volley (her weakest shot). She managed to put the ball on the strings, but her wrist twisted, and accordingly, the ball landed wide. The Abernathy's responded with celebratory fist pumps, as they now have match point.

As George eyed Ginnie, a throbbing pain coursed through his body in a distinctly north–south direction along the spine. With each passing moment, he could feel his movement become all the more restricted and wasn't sure how much longer he could keep his head from, well, oscillating.

As George glanced back at Ginnie, he noted that she was red-faced and flustered—a clear sign that not only was the pressure getting to her but that her mind was elsewhere. After several seconds of bouncing the ball, she served it into play, but the ball rocketed off Rose's strings right back at her. Ginnie managed to slice it back weakly, but unwittingly set the doctor up for an easy put-away. As the ball approached, Abernathy lined up it precisely. He then took, what George surmised, to be a perfect, textbook swing, but for some undefined reason or other, miss-hit the ball off the frame and it floated haphazardly toward

George. Taking a deep breath, George gingerly moved in to pick it off, but at the very last second, the ball clipped the net and unceremoniously drifted out of his reach, landing well within the baseline: the Abernathy's had defeated the Martians.

The Abernathy's, cock-a-hoop over their victory, celebrated with a series of whoops and high fives. They convened with their opponents for handshakes, but find they are a player short. Ginnie, who managed to offer what was, at best, lukewarm congratulations, now turned to look for George. In fact, they all began to look: in the far reaches of court five, near the rear entrance, spectators stood in little pools of disquiet as someone resembling him appeared to be, well, contorting himself. His arms, legs, and head twisted so spectacularly that one could not help but presume that he made his living as a world-class contortionist. Soon the crowd multiplied, taking on a paparazzi-like interest; it was as though at any moment, professional-grade cameras would emerge, complete with high-powered zoom lenses.

As Ginnie surveyed the scene, she had the look of one not fully able to digest the spectacle before her. She took a moment to watch as her husband's seemingly boneless, near completely malleable body morphed from one assorted posture to another, culminating in what can only be described as a human knot.

"George?"

From the ground of Court 5, George Martian remained silent. He was vaguely aware of his wife's presence, but was not, as of yet, inclined to hold up his end of the conversation. Instead, he did his best to look elsewhere, noting that Jenkins and the doctor were in consultation. At

153

length, Abernathy approached Ginnie with a touch of doctorly savvy.

"Your husband is having an allergic reaction to something," Abernathy said in no uncertain terms. "Likely from a pill of some sort."

Ginnie backed away in disbelief, as though she'd like nothing more than a second opinion. "George! You're not taking anything, are you? Are you?"

". . ."

"I'm asking you a question. George?"

George looked to Ginnie, then to Abernathy, and then back again to Ginnie. He repeated the pattern a handful of suspicious times, giving the impression of one who preferred to not speak openly.

With no response from George, Abernathy spoke with emergency room urgency:

"You appear to be having an allergic reaction of some kind, George. Depending on what you've taken, it could be fata-"

"Haldol. I'm taking Haldol," George said doing his very best to not look in Ginnie's direction.

In the minutes that passed, Abernathy gestured to Rose to retrieve his Benadryl—which, due to an aversion to bees, he never left home without. Seconds later, Abernathy emptied the bottle into George's mouth, all the while mumbling various medical terms: "tardive dyskinesia—a neurological disorder causing sustained muscle contractions . . . abnormal postures . . . involutary movements . . ." As he wiped George's mouth with his sleeve he continued, "Benadryl, the antidote."

At length, Ginnie emerged from her thoughts. She stepped toward George and proceeded to raise her eyebrows accusingly.

"Did your *mother* give them to you? Did she?"

". . ."

"George?"

"Yes," George confessed blinking his eyes wildly. "Yes, my mother gave me the pills."

Less than a second later Ginnie stormed off, saying nothing.

At a four-top corner table in the Grand Ballroom sat the Abernathy's and the Martians. The men and women talked among themselves in a state of connubial detachment. Amidst the food and wine, there was an element of cheer, an air, if you will, that all had been forgiven. With the arrival of more Cabernet, George was called upon for a toast. He rose to his feet gingerly, stiffly even—as though he'd recently endured some particularly hellish bodily assault. He held his glass at eye-level, as his wife, looking radiant, smiled upon him. George then cleared his throat and was about to speak when from across the room he spotted Glass. There was a look of panic about his face and as he neared, he broke into a series of wild hand gestures, as though trying to warn of something. It was then that George noticed a figure to his immediate left. Standing hipshot, was Mother.

CHAPTER 11: THE DOLLHOUSE

George stood a-smiling, just outside of handshaking distance, offering no more than the intermittent mono-syllable—trying, with all his might, *not* to look at his watch. Ginnie was giving him that look though: the one reserved for Sundays when they visited her parents. It was her dyed-in-wool look, an amalgam of squinted eyes and grimace, conveying, more or less, that he damn well better behave himself.

The visits themselves were arctic in length. The meal, like the conversation, both served and digested at a glacial pace. And George, frozen—a mere cog in the passing of time. For Sundays were all pageantry and long goodbyes.

The visits were a question not only of duration but also of frequency—as though there should exist a mathematical formula or algorithmic expression that took both holidays and birthdays into account and when computed, would arrive at a more reasonable (and undoubtedly lesser) number of visits. George actually tried to hammer it out a few times, even shared it with Ginnie. But ultimately, that meant limits. And when it came to her parents, there could be none. None.

They were positively friendless and gave him a near migraine on sight." *Mother* was corpulent and chub-faced, but always dressed to the nines. Imbued with a categorical aversion to anything on, or for the matter, near, the discount rack. Today, she wore a ribbon in her hair, tied with a precision, which in her mind, was deserving of nothing short of a standing ovation: as though if there were a contest, she'd not only be awarded grand prize, but deemed the official spokesperson. The rest of her ensemble (a housedress of sorts) was, by design, on the drab side, as it served only as a backdrop for the almighty ribbon.

They'd made the three-hour-long drive in silence. Sports radio their only sanity. It was like a funeral march, like being prodded before a firing squad. One, ostensibly, without blindfolds. Sometimes George would pray for an accident, for a careless driver or errant deer to pulverize them—to usher them to a *distant* hospital for weeks, months even. Instead they barreled down the turnpike unscathed.

As *Father*, or Claude, as he liked to be called, hobbled over to take their coats, George recalled their last visit: how the car battery had mysteriously died, and they had to spend the night. He remembered the blitzkrieg of fear and dread that overcame him. Of waking up at some ungodly hour and jump-starting the car to life. Of actually making it home before noon. And all of them—Ginnie included—thinking he'd done so out of the goodness of his heart: to spare Father from having to exert himself, for the man was only months removed from a double hip replacement. The man looked older now, George thought. Slumped. Dejected. Out of place on the loveseat, amongst *Mother's* dolls. The collection was her life's work, an omnium-gatherum of dolls of every kind. They had been at the center of an argument between husband and wife, the crux of which involved the dolls having to be moved in order to accommodate Claude. For it had been the only locale (outside of their bed) where the man, post-surgery, could lie comfortably. Still, Mother had made only the smallest of concessions, removing just three dolls: "No more." And so, the man spent his days sandwiched between an 8"-inch *Wendy Loves to Waltz* and a 21"-inch *Bride Lady of Fashion* under strict orders to not move, to not breathe, even in the slightest.

George sat now, hip-spread on a Morris chair, passing off an expression of one having a swell time. The others were opposite him on a loveseat, with Ginnie customarily in the middle.

"So, a new doll Bessie, huh?" George asked, addressing his mother-in-law.

"Yes, George. Yes"," the woman said, unable to hide her pleasure. Then, with an air of dramatics, she raised the doll in question from her lap and did a sort of two-handed trophy pose: "It's a vintage Madame Alexander! Been looking for one my *whole* life!"

George smiled back broadly, making sure Ginnie could see his efforts. On the coffee table between them lay an impressive stack of photo albums.

"I've never really collected anything," George said, doing his best to hold up his end of the conversation. "I used to have quite a few baseball car"-"

"Your father and I cleaned out the attic the other day," Mrs. Martian interrupted. She then gave her daughter a proprietary look and said, "Thought it be fun to look through them."

George sat back in the chair and sighed heavily, knowing full well what was to come. He then watched as his 28-year-old wife morphed, face and all, into a schoolgirl: "Sure, Mommy!" she said in a little kid voice.

"Sounds like fun!"

Her father then picked up the top album and said happily, "Let's start with this one!"

For the next hour, George watched as the threesome poured over photo album after photo album—recounting bygone days, reminiscing.

"What about this one? Do you remember that?" George's mother-in-law asked her daughter rather excitedly. She was pointing at a photo George could not exactly see, but for which the lace cover read, "Girl Scouts."

"Yes, of course I remember," Ginnie said. "How could I forget? That was the year you were the 'cookie mom.'"

"You were an absolute doll in that outfit"," the girl's father said.

George watched the girl's mother lean forward; she said elaborately, "I found it you know. I should really show it to you."

"My Girl Scout uniform?" Ginnie asked. "Would love to see it!"

Something now, and quickly, darted across the room: Mabel, the family's prized miniature poodle, dressed in his very own tuxedo. As though in a fit of protest, she bolted onto the dining room table and proceeded to dismantle Mother's table setting: flatware, glassware, calligraphied place cards were upturned in matter of seconds. There were sounds that one remembers that never quite escape one's head, and for George, the shriek that Mother emitted happened to be just that: a cagey staccato with an aliveness all its own reverberated through the house, its owner pausing just long enough to *command* the others to intervene. Moments later, by means of any number of hands, the canine was banished to the snowmelt that was the backyard.

A tantrum ensued as Mother flounced off to the bedroom. Father trailed behind, his cadence managing to be both subservient and crab-like. There was, for George, something altogether admirable about her actions: an ability to lash out, to let loose—that he, for the better part of his life, had never quite managed. As a child, he'd been raised to never make a "scene." That such displays were "low brow" and "unseemly," reserved—as his mother would say—for those who "didn't know any better." Still, as he watched the efficient woman in the scarf storm about the room, he could not help but wonder what such a release might feel like.

As George and Ginnie worked to reset the table, unruly happenings emerged from the innerworkings of the house. Between the sobbing and wails came the throwing of objects, the shattering of mirrors.

"You don't have to do this, you know"," George said, looking Ginnie squarely in the eye.

Ginnie sat down a glass pitcher and gave George a look that defied clemency. "Do what?"

George approached Ginnie and grabbed her hard at the elbow. It was as though he was overcome by some naked, human force.

"Stop it, will ya?" he demanded. "It's been going on long enough."

Ginnie gave a cursory look to the staircase and then turned back to George. "Now isn't the time, George. Besides, Mother is *already* upset. I can't let them down now. I can't deny them."

There was a spangle of a tear rolling down Ginnie's face, and George reached out and wiped it away. "This is the last time," he said unequivocally. "Understand me? One way or the other, this is the *absolute* last time."

They dined now, or rather, snacked on the latest offerings from *Cooking Light* magazine: water chestnuts, bamboo shoots, tomato-basil skewers. Compliments large and small filtered the host's' way over bowls of cold cucumber soup. While three-quarters of the table chin-wagged over the finer points of doll collecting, George silently two-handed his Sango Nova bowl, scanning the table for salt. He then recalled that salt and, for that matter, pepper were for all intents and purposes unavailable, for seasoning of any kind was construed as nothing short of sacrilege. An outright insult to Mother's cooking. He'd made the mistake of asking for butter years ago and upon Mother storming out, was told in effect by the rest of the table that none was necessary. That *everything* from the corn-on-the-cob to the dinner rolls was already perfect. Perfect.

Presently, George sat at the dinner table with his hands folded, taking stock, cataloging—systematically bracing himself for what was about to happen. He then watched as his mother-in-law nodded at Ginnie, and in the next instant, his wife of three years, abruptly and familiarly, did her best approximation of an unruly child.

Ginnie slumped low in her chair, such that the tip of her nose was just visible over the tabletop. She then laughed heartily and chanted, "I'm not hungry! I'm not hungry!" in a voice that was unmistakably that of a 9-year-old.

"Stop that right this instant!" the girl's mother said as she clapped her hands.

"I want ice cream!" the girl repeated, slumping even lower in the chair. *"I want ice cream!"*

Just then George watched his father-in-law drop his fork with a matter-of-fact plop. "Listen to your mother!" he said. "Now, sit up straight. Now!"

Ginnie obliged, but rolled her eyes and giggled as though reminding everyone that she remained very much in the throes of girlhood. She proceeded to make a show of fussing with her hair and biting her nails before being told, in effect, to stop the monkey business. Minutes passed and then, without pretext, Ginnie belched.

"That's it! To the corner!" the girl's mother commanded. Compliantly, Ginnie rose to her feet.

It was a little game they played. One George had witnessed countless times before, but never truly managed to wrap his mind around. The best he'd managed to gather was that it was a payment of sorts—for Ginnie having married, for having, well, grown up.

As Ginnie passed him, George held his breath, fearing that if he exhaled, she would permanently topple over. And just like every time before, they exchanged the briefest of glances—a sort of dialogue of the eyes, subtle contortions of the face that hearten him, but ultimately hold no answers.

It had taken George the better part of their marriage to straighten her out. To get her to the point that she could both see and hear the world without her parents' narration. Yet even now, despite his best efforts, there were these moments of treachery—episodes, if you will, that kept her in a kind of servitude, a parental mind-lock.

Ginnie, sour and inconsolable, chewed at her sleeves.

As *Bette Midler: Greatest Hits* played through for no

less than the fourth time, the main course was served: Chicken with dried plums and sage, a side of spinach-feta turnovers. They ate in silence with one seat open, for Ginnie remained in the corner.

"I'm sorry, Mother. I'm sorry, father"," Ginnie sobbed in a voice that was unmistakably that of repentant child.

George watched his in-laws consult one another, and after a moment Mother said, "Do you promise to behave yourself?"

"Yes"," the girl said, "I promise."

"Alright then," Mother said, "but this is your last chance."

Atop the dining room table sat an oversized centerpiece of bird-of-paradise flowers, arranged with an exactness that rendered them a virtual ornament to themselves. From over the flora George was able to just make out the three people sitting on the *opposite* side of the table. He watched them bob their heads, noting that Ginnie was crying, though he could not say for sure.

At length, elaborate desserts were served: Bananas Foster, Vanilla Biscotti, Autumn Maple Cookies, but upon George they had little effect. He declined offers of coffee and tea, and soon retreated to the confines of his thoughts.

When they'd first married, there'd been a number of incidents. Behaviors, which over the years, he'd for the most part put a stop to. How he'd routinely arrive home from work only to find Ginnie sitting in complete dark, her body curled listlessly around the phone as Mother, by the hour, fed her more poison.

There had also been the matter of Christmas gifts, or rather, gifts in general. How Ginnie had gone to great lengths to conceal anything she'd received from his side of the family. As though the very act of unwrapping the item or items in question was tantamount to betraying her family. The last draw had come when she'd gone so far as to deposit an antique vase from George's uncle into a nearby snowbank.

The incident had been resolved through untold hours of intervention. George had explained, in no uncertain terms, that he loved her and that she was, in his eyes, the perfect embodiment of woman. That, save for this "parent fixation," they had everything going for them. Everything. But it hadn't been his words that convinced her, rather those of her favorite author. The book had been sitting on the coffee table when George had knocked it over (for she always kept it within arm's reach). Reflexively, he'd picked it up and was about to set it down when his eyes passed over a page, 106. Mid-paragraph. Eleven lines down, to be exact. George had read it to himself at first, and then, on something less than a whim, began to recite aloud:

A child is a guest in the house, to be loved and respected, never possessed.

Over and over again George's voice grew louder with each repetition. Ginnie had stood there, deaf and unthinking, as though what was being said was of no more consequence than a stranger reciting his grocery list. But then, after forty some repetitions, she surrendered: falling into his arms, a waterfall of tears.

As was custom, the women disappeared to the upper floor of the house, playing, what was for all intents and purposes, an elaborate game of dress up. When they returned, Ginnie was dressed in a green-and-khaki number, complete with assorted badges, a sash, and a beret: for Mother had decked Ginnie out in her old Girl Scout uniform. Had it been the first time, it would have made for a shocking bit of footage, but instead there was for George only a vague sense of hopelessness, a realization along the width and narrow of his mind that while something was terribly wrong, he was powerless. For in the three years of his marriage, he'd said nothing, and had, for some undefined reason, stomached it. But now, as he watched Mother fuss with Ginnie's beret as though she were a *doll*, a sensation was rising—a feeling, he was beginning to sense, he could no longer suppress.

"You look positively adorable!" Mother exclaimed as Ginnie paraded about the center of the living room.

Ginnie looked at her mother, bright and expectant, the way only a schoolgirl could: "Thank you, Mother," she replied and did a little twirl. "Thank you!"

"It's a good thing you've kept your figure"," Father interjected from the antiqued confines of a rocking chair. "Otherwise, your mother might've had to get out the thread and needle!"

"Thank you, Father. Thank you"," Ginnie replied, this time offering a curtsey.

George watched as his mother-in-law and father-in-law beamed with pride. It was hard for him to tell which of them was enjoying this more. He tried to get Ginnie's attention, but as was the case in such instances, she could never look him in the eye.

"Excuse me, little girl"," father said with a wry smile, "are you selling cookies again this year?" Then without waiting for a response he asked, "Do you have any Tagalongs?"

Ginnie looked at her father wide-eyed. She then made

a frown of her face and, playing along raised the palms of her hands upward. "Sorry, sir," she said with a shrug, "but I'm fresh out."

In the next instant, the parentals erupted in a tide of applause—George, the sole non-participant, just sat. There were other outfits, of course: Ginnie's parochial school uniform, the one from her dance recital, the dress from her Sweet 16 party, and with each passing, headfucking Sunday, she'd indulge her parents and try a few on—infantilizing herself as George hopelessly looked on.

From the bay window, George fumed, taking in pockets of hot, nervous breath. Behind him, Ginnie was now in the midst of reciting the Girl Scout's oath. Her right hand was raised in the prototypical oath-like manner, but the cracks in her speaking voice betrayed the sentiment.

"The Girl Scout Promise is the way Girl Scouts agree to act every day toward one another and other people"," Ginnie recited. "The Girl Scout *Law* outlines a way to act toward one another and the world."

"Don't forget the last part," Mother advised, from the far reaches of the davenport. "You *always* forget the last part."

Ginnie stood in the center of the room, quivering—as though forever encumbered by the trappings of her childhood. She took a breath, fought off a wave of tears, and then mustered a winning smile.

"On my honor, I will try to serve God and my country!" she announced.

"And?" her father said.

Ginnie closed her eyes hard, but the tears could be held back no more. "And my parents!" Ginnie added quietly.

"Louder," Mother commanded.

Ginnie teetered for moment, her oath-hand shaking immoderately in the living room air. "And my parents!" she repeated loudly and sank on the davenport.

"Marvelous, dear! Just marvelous!" Mother exclaimed, and rose to her feet.

From a distance, George watched Ginnie wipe at her eyes once more, her parents seemingly unwilling or unable to acknowledge her tears. "Thank you, Mother!" she said and forced a smile. "That's-That's nice of you to say."

"How 'bout one more?" her father asked, looking in the direction of his wife for approval.

With a wide smile, the woman moved in the direction of the stairs and said excitedly, "I think the ballerina tutu would just about top the day!" Behind her, Ginnie and Father followed.

Outside everything was grey and snowmelt, Mabel nowhere in sight. As George glanced down and to his right, his eyes passed over the innumerable dolls. He studied their prettied faces and, for the first time, became horrifyingly aware of their striking resemblance to Ginnie: baby dolls, infants, prepubescent girls—fixed life stages, capturing a bygone time.

Somewhere along the width and narrow of his mind, he knew he should've been firm-footed and put a stop to the madness. Truth was, it disarmed him, such that he watched "proceedings" play out for years with low to moderate interest, remaining neutral and affectless. But the redoubtable fact was that by remaining actionless, he'd perpetuated it. Ginnie had other sisters, of course. A progeny of four, who, due to being some ten years older, had long since made their getaway, leaving an infant Ginnie behind. She'd thus grown up in familial seclusion, with all that she saw and experienced narrated and interpreted by her parents. She'd had no other conceivable reference point. For deep in Ginnie's head was an undermemory: a perception that her parents were embodied with some junked-up form of saintliness, as though they were a pair of infallible lifeforms. And that if she did not abide by them, she would suffer some giant unknoweable loss. But it was false, a mere trickery of human-craft designed to keep her in their fortress. What she needed was a counterforce. A defender. Something she had not possessed, till now:

George remembered closing the blinds, of actually slamming them shut. And all of them running—running to see what he'd done: torn, shredded, disembodied; dollparts that were dolls no more.

"A child is a guest in the house, to be loved and respected, never possessed," George shouted as the threesome bounded down the stairs.

There was a look of abject horror on Mother's face: "What! What have you done?" she shouted as her head swiveled over the remains of the dolls.

Ignoring his mother-in-law, George bolted over to Ginnie, who was dressed in her pinkish tutu, and hooked his arm around her. He gave her a brief look and then turned back to face Ginnie's parents.

George looked over at his father-in-law; his mouth was open, but only just. "A child is a guest in the house," George said resolutely, "to be loved and respected, never possessed!"

"Stop this! Stop this madness," Mother demanded as she crouched over the remains of her Madame Alexander.

George grabbed hold of Ginnie's hand, and, in return, she squeezed his tight.

"A child is a guest in the house, to be loved and respected, never possessed," they said in unison.

"My God! Can't you see what you've done!" Father shouted as though he'd just now recovered his speaking voice.

"You've gone and ruined them all!" Mother shouted, still crouched over.

"A child is a guest in the house, to be loved and respected, never possessed," they repeated.

"How dare you!" Mother yelled with venom, looking George directly in the eye. "How dare you do this to my family! How dare you do this to my little girl."

George watched Ginnie bring a finger to her lips and promptly shush him. In the next instant, it was Ginnie's voice alone:

"I'm not a little girl, anymore, Mother and Father," Ginnie said. "I'm not a little girl anymore and I'll have no more of this!"

George watched as the parentals stared back—there was a vague look of forlornness on their faces, but nothing more.

"Mother? Father?" Ginnie repeated. "I said I'm all grown up and I'll have no more of this."

George watched Ginnie as she waited for a response, but none came. In the next instant, her parents silently dropped to their knees and busily worked at salvaging the dolls.

"A child is a guest in the house," Ginnie said, "to be loved and respected, never possessed."

George stood for moment in the stunted stillness of the

room and gazed at the couple for the last time. Then, with a connubial tug on Ginnie's sleeve, they were out the door.

CHAPTER 12: THE MASTER PLAN

Before George even reached the bus parking lot that day, he'd already made up his mind: the woman had to go. He'd been contemplating it for some time, but this last exchange had finally put him over. Five years was enough. Hell, more than enough. The trouble was, it was nearly impossible to get rid of staff, even those of low status. He would have to do something bold. Underhanded. Risky. If he was caught, it would likely be the end of his career. However, if it came down to his word against hers, it wasn't even close. For he was a member of the faculty in good standing. He served on numerous committees, including heading up Honor Society, the Debate team, the Chess club and the Scholarship Board.

Despite Ms. Chase's peculiarities, she was remarkable with children. She embodied all the qualities a "classroom helper" should have. The trouble, at least in George's estimate, was that she was forever running from her past, and just as quickly, from the present—thus rendering herself in a constant state of hysteria, which came in the form of paranoia one day, and delusion the next: there was the time she dialed 911 because she heard a bomb ticking; there was the time she had seen Russian paratroopers dropping from the sky; there was the time a UFO had followed her to work. Then there were the transgressions against George himself: there was the time she informed the class of his exact salary (how she knew this was beyond him); there was the time she told the class that the reason he was accident prone was because he was Polish; there was the time she confided to her cheerleading squad that even if George were single, he was "'a bit pudgy for her tastes.'" She did not speak these words out of malice, but for the simple reason that she firmly and wholeheartedly believed them to be true. And in George's mind, this meant only one thing: she was mad.

Adding to George's predicament were the events of a month ago: he'd been sitting at his desk grading papers when he felt something in his lap. It felt like a child, and in many ways it was. Ms. Chase was in complete hysterics. Between the fits of crying and the occasional nose blow, Ms. Chase revealed she'd been having a dalliance with a staff member, who had just that morning broken it off. She never disclosed whom, nor did George much care, but what he did care about was her sudden change in behavior: from that day forward she no longer left the room. Not even for the bathroom. It was maddening. In the past, George had counted on and, in fact, encouraged, her to take as many breaks for as long as she liked. It was these minutes of solitude that kept him going. He had to have them. Upon further investigation, George learned a few other notables: Ms. Chase parked in a different lot; she entered the building through the rear entrance; she would go nowhere near the main office.

In the weeks that followed, Ms. Chase was ever present. George tried getting her to run meaningless errands or make unnecessary copies, but every time he made a request, she was instantly petrified. It wasn't just Ms. Chase's endless chatter that was intolerable, but the questions. What had he had for dinner? Was it good? What TV show did he watch? What time did he go to bed? Day after day it was the same mindless conversation. He tried getting her assigned to study hall duty, but the minute he mentioned her name to Principal Thurmer, he would hear nothing of it. And then, one day, in the midst of a particularly grueling session, something occurred to him that for some reason had never occurred to him before: if she wouldn't leave the room, he would. It was liberating. Initially, he just roamed the halls, but eventually stumbled upon the bus parking lot. It was quiet. He could think. Even take one of his pills, if he was feeling a bit "'jumpy.'" It became his only escape. And so, each and every day, when he could simply take no more of the woman, he went to the bus lot. It became his salvation.

Presently, George leaned up against the rear door of the bus garage fondling his pill box. With exception to the odd chain-smoking mechanic or bus driver, the area was entirely his own. He stood for moment in the sunglow, dim-eyed and reasoning, knowing full well that these were the good days. Mother had signed over the house just last week, once official news of the twins had come to light. And this Dr. Seabring fellow seemingly had him on a good mental path: a combination of twice-a-week therapy sessions and innumerable prescriptions that had him in a near-normal state, not to mention sleeping. Now, if only this situation with Ms. Chase could be resolved, things would very nearly be peachy.

George watched as a bus driver strolled by carrying a wrench. He nodded at George and George nodded back, and in the next instant, the man in the Dickie jumpsuit disappeared. A second later, George brought a yellow legal pad he'd had wedged between ribcage and armpit out in front of him and sat down on a misplaced folding chair. For the briefest of seconds, he recalled the ungodly number of folding chairs he'd sat in over the years at the talent shows, and in response, expelled a purely private, inside-joke laugh. After a moment of looking sunward, George pulled out his engraved Cross pen and began to write, employing his left thigh of course, as a makeshift desk. The top sheet read, "Master Plan," and what followed was a list of schemes George had devised to rid himself of Ms. Chase. Initially, he'd devised pages of them, but eventually whittled the best ones down a single sheet. He didn't like the guesswork involved. Something might go wrong anywhere along the line, but that was the nature of the businesses. While he remained undecided on precisely which tactic to employ, one thing he knew for sure was the time. It would be on the last day of school. That way, should something go wrong, he would at least have summer to recover, or worse, look for a new job.

For the next half hour, George poured over his collective work, writing, rewriting, and crossing out various schemes. There were margin notes, scribbles, arrows, and the like covering the page, such that George decided to rewrite his best ideas into a clean, fresh sheet. When he was at last done, he allowed himself to smile and rose to a standing position, breathing in pockets of gull-fresh air. Teaching may not have been his ideal profession, he thought, but it had indeed grown on him. Like most things, it had been his mother's idea: "good hours, summers off, and a pension that cannot be beat," were her words verbatim, and he had to admit, she had undoubtedly been right. But there was also something undeniable about his students: they were open-eyed and clear-souled with noggin upon noggin of untapped grey matter to boot. And while he was no longer in receivership of trophies and ovations, at least he still had a stage.

As George reentered the first floor of Milburn Academy, he paused mid-stride to make sure a certain document of the top-secret variety was properly secured. He was feeling good. Giddy even. Rounding the corner, he chanced upon a giant atrium-style mirror. He'd passed countless times before, but something about it today gave him pause: he saw his full profile from head to foot, and there, lying dormant, was a foreboding presence, some unnameable threat. Seconds later, he hot-footed it down the hallway, hoping in his heart of hearts it was bad lighting or an aberration.

It was the last day of school at Milburn Academy— teachers and staff were strewn about the building, some in the halls, some in their classrooms, and some in the faculty lounge. On this particular morning, 7:42 a.m. to be exact, George Martian plodded away at his desk. Sports radio played while he read intently. It was quiet now. It was just the way he liked it.

The room itself was elaborately decorated and, oddly, had a feminine touch. There was also an overpowering smell of perfume. As George circled something in red, he consulted the wall clock. He then took a sip of coffee and braced himself for what was about to happen, and then, as if on cue, he heard high heels bounding down the hall: they were not a comfortable stride, but instead had a frantic quality. In his last moments of peace, George's stuffed the small of papers he'd been working on in his desk.

Ms. Chase entered at an alarming rate. She held a thermos of coffee in one hand and a bottle of water in the other. From each shoulder hung a purse, and under one arm, was a half-eaten bagel sandwich. She was on the verge of dropping everything. While her legs seemed up to the task, her arms trembled. Teetering, she hurried past George and made it to her desk just in time. Through a mouthful of Bubblicious, she said, "Good morning," and then she was off, for there is much for her to do: it was a spectacle George had witnessed countless times, but one he could never pull his eyes from. She began by straightening all twenty-two desks, which in George's estimation looked fine to begin with. She then smoothed out the many posters (some of which are quite high and require her to climb a rather steep bookcase). Returning to ground level, she raced to the bulletin board and rearranged its contents; at the windows, she adjusted the blinds until they were perfectly symmetrical. From there, she darted to the blackboard and proceeded to write the date with surprising vigor, only to erase it and write it again. At her desk, she took a much-deserved swig of coffee, but before taking a seat, she watered her prized spider plant (it was of such proportion that it not only occupied her desk but also encroached on a good portion of George's). In the eleven years they had worked together, she not once neglected the plant. She even came in on the weekends to care for it. As for George, he regarded it in the same manner as his "colleague": a monstrosity.

Presently, the sounding of the bell has unleashed a seemingly endless wave of students. By this time, Ms. Chase has assumed her customary position just outside of the classroom. As she leaned against the wall and applied a new coat of lipstick, a sign on the door, which read, MR. MARTIAN & MS. CHASE, fell to the floor. She attempted to pick it up, but the myriad of children made it difficult. From a crouched position, she darted in and out of the swarm. After a few tries, she managed to grab a corner, but as she picked it up, a size-six Reebok pulled it from her grip: the tear going right through her name.

Back in the room, George opened a window. The pesticide of a perfume was already getting to his head. As Ms. Chase entered, he noticed that she appeared to be on the verge of crying. Worse yet, she'd made eye contact:

"Where are the kids?" she asked, dabbing at her eyes.

"Zoo. Field trip."

Ms. Chase plopped into her desk chair, "How's come we're not going?"

Ever the grammarian, George cringed, "How's come?"

"Yeah, how's come?"

"Thought it best if we stayed back," George answered and abruptly became preoccupied with his desk calendar.

Ms. Chase looked sad and offered a barely audible, "Oh."

The truth was George had done everything he could to get the train (wreck) on the bus. However, it was a popular trip, and by the time he actually read the flier, all chaperone spots had been filled. As George fussed with bending a rather temperamental paperclip back into submission, he felt a pair of eyes staring him down no less than three feet away.

"Do you like monkeys?" Ms. Chase asked, straight-faced.

George looked up from the paperclip he was holding and squinted his eyes. He felt as though he was losing IQ points by the second. "What's that?"

"Monkeys, silly, do you like them?"

George set down the paperclip and swiveled his chair a

few degrees to his right. Then, from a deep, retentive portion of his head, he cerebrated over the utter randomness of Ms. Chase's question: "I suppose."

"'Cause I love them! Don't you just love them?"

Before he responded, George noted the woman's eyes were still watered up, and so, with the hope of avoiding an all-out meltdown, he said rather cheerfully: "I suppose I do! I do love the monkeys!"

Over the next few minutes, a litany of end-of-year announcements came over the P.A. followed by the Pledge of Allegiance. When the "'broadcast,'" as George liked to call it, had concluded, he sat down in his chair and swiveled such that his back was facing Ms. Chase. He then began the task of clearing off his desk, in lieu of summer vacation.

Seconds later, from a point just over his shoulder, he heard Ms. Chase's voice call out: "Did'ja want me to grade these?"

George gave a quick, cursory look at the spelling quizzes Ms. Chase was holding and then turned away. "Sure."

Ms. Chase cleared her throat. "Well, I can do them now or after lunch."

"Either," George said as he opened a desk drawer and tossed his stapler inside.

"Well, I can do them now or after lunch," she repeated.

George closed the drawer hard. "It doesn't matter."

"Well, I can do them now or after lunch," "she said once more.

George expelled a sigh and abruptly spun his chair toward Ms. Chase. "Grade them," he said. Then for emphasis, he added, "Now."

Ms. Chase then picked up her red pen, but couldn't

locate the answer key.

"Um . . . Mr. Martian?" she said with an air of helplessness.

George gripped a number 2 pencil in his left hand till it snapped. "Yes?"

"Where's the answer key?"

George dropped the remains of the pencil into a garbage bin, but refused to turn around. "On your desk." He could hear a frantic shuffling of papers behind him and clenched his eyes tight. "It's under the plant."

"Don't. See. It," she said in a sing-song voice.

George swiveled around in his chair noting Ms. Chase had lifted up her purse. "I said under the plant, not your purse."

Ms. Chase dropped the purse she had pinched between her fingers and then lifted up her other, secondary purse: "Not here!"

"George turned his neck slightly, such that Ms. Chase came into full view. "No, not the purse, the plant," he clarified.

Ms. Chase dropped the second purse and proceeded to sift through a stack of multiplication flashcards. "Not here!"

"I SAID UNDER THE PLANT! THE PLANT!" George said, his voice more than slightly agitated.

Ms. Chase lifted up a few extraneous branches of her beloved plant and giggled, "Oh!" she exclaimed. "There it is!"

George wiped a patch of sweat from his forehead and expelled a few breaths. As painful as this exchange had been, there were many others. But the one that came to George's mind now was the one that had set him on his current course of action. It had been exactly two months ago. He had just returned from a sick day. His first in years:

"Feeling better?"

"Yes, thanks."

"Go to the doctor?"

"No."

"No?"

"No."

"Silly! How's come?"

"I'm really feeling much better," George had said dismissively and went directly to his desk. "Thanks."

"Hope so, really hope so."

And then, just when George had turned away and busied himself with something extremely pressing, she'd continued:

"By the way, if you don't mind me asking, are ya on any meds?"

"Huh?"

"Cuz I happened to see you standing in line at the pharmacy. Looked like you had one for your wife, too. That right?"

Before George had responded, he remembered he'd fantasized: not of sex, but pure Tarantino-like violence. Usually, he envisioned taking an excellent hole puncher to the half-wit. But like always, he'd showcased restraint.

"We're all doing fine," he'd said. "Thanks."

"Cuz I thought I heard the pharmacist say something about . . . you know, if your wife was a little yeasty or something? She should really get that checked out."

At that point, George had actually picked up the hole puncher, thought about it, and walked out.

Presently, Ms. Chase was working feverishly on a new

sign. She sat at her desk surrounded by a heap of markers, a ruler, and what appeared to be a container of glitter. She was determined. It wasn't until George noticed the flowers surrounding his name that he knew it was time.

"You know," "he said diplomatically, "it is the *last* day of school we probably don't need a new sign."

"Yeah, I know," Ms. Chase said without bothering to look up, "but it just seemed *so* sad . . . I'll just make a new one."

George looked to his left and to his right as though concerned that an outside party might be in earshot. He then leaned over to Miss Chase and said rather cryptically, "By the by, I don't know if you've heard, but there's a chance we won't even be in this room next year."

Ms. Chase dropped the container of glitter she'd been holding and looked up at George, wide-eyed. "What?"

"What I mean is, with the summer renovation, there's a good chance we won't be in this room. Heck, there's a good chance we won't be working together."

"HUH?"

George looked the woman squarely in the eye, knowing full well he had her. "Well, I didn't want to bring this up, but there's the distinct possibility that teaching classroom helpers could be reassigned."

Ms. Chase stared back; her mouth was open, but only just. "Reassigned?"

George fought off a smile, all the while doing his best to convey a tone of bad news. "Well, yes," "he said. "You see, I happened to be in the main office the other day and overheard something—I'd rather not say who—but it sounds like it's going to happen."

"Going to happen?"

George again looked to his left and to his right. "Listen," he said in a whisper. "I didn't want to upset you, but thought you ought to know."

When George saw the tears, a small but perceptible sensation of guilt overcame him, and in the next instant, he handed over his handkerchief. Ms. Chase gave a blow and handed it back before speaking.

"Oh, Mr. Martian, what should I do?" she said dabbing at the corner of her eyes.

"Do you *really* want my advice?"

"Yes!"

"And I can trust you that this will remain confidential? You realize the position I'd be putting myself in?"

"Oh, absolutely I'd never do anything-"

"Alright then, what you need to do is march down to administration and request a placement change."

Ms. Chase raised her eyebrows almost to the point that they formed question marks. "A placement change?"

"Yes," George said. "What you need to do is tell them that you must be reassigned to another teacher."

"Another teacher?"

George shook his head back and forth in a manner that implied sympathy, and then looked at Ms. Chase. "I realize it will be a tough adjustment, but at least this way you'll have a choice."

"A choice?"

"Yes, you wouldn't want to get stuck with old Maureen or Vargas would you?"

Ms. Chase grimaced as though she suddenly had a bad taste in her mouth. "Oh, that'd be horrible!"

George smiled. "Indeed it would. Just tell Principal Thurmer there is a personality conflict that is negatively impacting the children."

Ms. Chase bowed her head as though she'd just been found out. "Oh, I could never do that."

"Why not, my dear?"

"Thurmer? Thurmer?"

As Ms. Chase's face continued to redden, it slowly dawned on George—she'd been fooling around with old Thurmer. *He* was the reason she no longer left the room. *He* was the reason his own solitude had disappeared. Realizing this monumental oversight, George felt all manner of hope slip away: he had failed. *All* the hours he'd spent planning had gone to waste. It had all been for naught. Gritting his teeth, George suddenly felt the need for one of his many pills. And so, without warning, he bolted from his desk. There was only one place for him to go.

Rosemary Chase once again found herself alone. She could never understand Mr. Martian's sudden departures, but she was sure he had a good reason. After all, he was a teacher. *He* was important. She sat at her desk, chewing at her fingernails, doing everything she could to avoid the present. It was too much for her. She had to escape, if only for a few moments. It was time for a little mischief. She closed the door, turned off the lights, and sat at George's desk. It was a *teacher* desk, and though it was identical to hers, she found that this one had a luxurious, powerful quality. She took a moment to swivel in the teacher chair and even giggled. She was already feeling better. She then moved on to George's desk calendar. Meetings. Appointments. Boring. She then opened up his Grossman's planner and began to rifle through it. It was more than a planner, however, for George had a tendency to throw in old receipts and make diary-like notations. It was where the good stuff was. Going page by page, she confirmed the following: George was again behind on his mortgage, he'd recently gotten a parking ticket, and that his wife indeed had a yeast infection (and judging by the dosage, an apparently furious one). Satisfied, she put everything back in place and was about to get up when she noticed a piece of paper sticking out of the main drawer. Normally, it would not have caught her attention, but it was on yellow legal paper, not the standard white loose-leaf that the children used. She couldn't resist.

When George returned, he found the room strangely empty. Then he saw it: on Ms. Chase's desk sat a single sheet of yellow legal paper. *His* yellow legal paper. At the top, written in his signature block lettering were the words, "Master Plan." What followed was mostly crossed out, except for one section. It was circled in red and was barely legible. It detailed something bold. Something under-handed. Something risky:

#8 Convince Ms. Chase to ask for placement change. She will dread being placed with old Maureen or Vargas. MAKE IT SO!

As panic set in, George paced wildly around the room. His job would be gone. So would his pension. Who would hire him now? And what about the twins that were on the way? The twins! As these thoughts and many others reeled through his head, George noticed the trail of leaves and potting soil that littered the floor. They seemed to form a trail out the door. The plant was gone. In the five years they'd shared a room, it had not been moved, and if the plant was gone, it was gone for good, and that could only mean one thing. Gone too was its owner.

CHAPTER 13: THE COMPANION

George lay in bed with his eyes wide open, a down comforter draped just under his chapped upper lip. The twins were asleep a bedroom over, and next to him, paradoxically, so too was his wife. He'd been frittering away in bed for hours—his beloved cocktail of pills seemingly no longer able to put him out. As he stared at the ceiling, the way slumberers-in-reverse were prone to do, he felt his mind pulsate at an irregular rhythm, almost as though he would at any moment mentally untether.

All at once George sat up in bed, pulled back the comforter, and stood up in the 2:40 a.m. darkness. As he gazed down at Ginnie, he desperately wanted to wake her; he wanted to do something, hell, *anything*, to put an end to the aloneness. He'd been sleepless now for a full week, the worst bit of insomnia he'd known since his university days. He was resigned to the exhaustion, to the somnolent eyes, but the hours of tossing and turning each night while everyone else slept, left him, well, reeling.

With his head craned at his wife, the motorized breeze of a non-oscillating fan brought a chill to his boxer-short-only legs. As George reached out a hand to wake Ginnie, he paused and took in the full array of her slumber: for the next few minutes he studied her face as though in search of some naked human truth, but finding none, dropped his hand to his side. Just then, a pill-induced stomach cramp that he'd been fighting off for past hour overtook him, and in response, he abruptly rose to his feet and hot-footed toward the master bathroom.

A moment later, George settled himself on the toilet and picked up the latest issue of *Time* magazine. The subscription had been a gift from Mother, to take his mind off things—to make him more worldly, more external. It was the December 18, 2006, "Person of the Year" issue, the cover depicting a keyboard with a mirror for a computer screen—a bold, perhaps clever, commentary on the celebration of self. As George shifted the magazine between his hands to get a better look, he found that the bulb above caused a watty glare to form across the mirrored portion— and in that instant the light was especially flattering, setting his reflection aglow. And there on the front cover, *he* was: his companion. Staring. Rubbernecking. George smiled and his reflection smiled back, and all at once, in one great rattle-banging moment, he was sane no more.

"Hello," George said.

"Hello to you, too," his companion replied.

It was a face well worth beholding, George thought, and as he watched the saccade of companion's eyes match his, he was agog.

"What's-What's your name?" George asked sheepishly.

The rictus of the face staring back at George frowned as though put off by the question. "Name?" I have no name."

George adjusted the magazine between his hands and brought the mirrored portion inches from his face. "Then who the hell are you?"

"I'm your companion, George," his reflection said as the face in the mirror broke out into a wide smile. "*Your* companion."

George closed his eyes and looked away as though with but a perfunctory turn of the head he could fight off the madness.

"What are you doing here?" George asked when he, at last, opened his eyes. "Where did you come from?"

"I've always been here, George"," his companion explained. "Always. The only difference is that you're *finally* paying attention."

George cleared his throat as though speaking in two distinct voices was a trifle much for his vocal chords. "I don't understand," George said shaking his head sideways. "I'm very, very conf-"

"I'm here for *you*, George," the companion interrupted. "That's *all* you really need to know. I'm here for *you*."

There was a lilting, sing-song quality to his companion's voice that reminded George of his dead father, and as that singular bit of recognition percolated through his neurals, he dropped his face into his hands and cried.

"I want you to look at me, George"," his companion said several minutes later. "I mean *really* look at me."

George lifted his head and looked into his companion's eyes. They were brown just like his. Hell, the whole face was the same. But somehow the profile opposite him resonated more, carried more weight, and as George blinked his eyes, it seemed to have a dominion over him.

"You and I are infrangible, George"," his companion declared. "Infrangible. Do you know what that means?"

George nodded his head, "Yes."

"Good, George. Good"," his companion said. "Now I want to tell you something, okay?"

George again nodded his head, hanging on to every word.

"I love you, George," his companion emoted. "And I want you to love me. Do you love me, George? Do you?"

Sweat purled off George's head and he took a moment to wipe it away. "Yes," he replied. "Yes! I love you!"

"Alright then."

First, there was a hand in George's lap and then down the front of his briefs. Playful flirting ensued and the courtship was underway. George found he could not help himself from ogling. He was especially fond of the companion's dundrearies and those big brown eyes. In the next instant, they were kissing, embracing. At length, the dirty talk began and soon they were *both* aroused. The love-making moved at a breakneck pace—the near-violent gyrations rendering George bruised and chafed. After climaxing, they splayed themselves out on the bathroom and, accordingly, 'spooned. Before they could get too comfortable though, George could hear Ginnie's approaching footsteps and after whispering something to his new friend, he abruptly stood up and flushed the toilet.

"George? You in there? What in God's name are you doing?"

George cleared his throat and deep-sixed the magazine behind the toilet. "Nothing," he said, "just under the weather is all."

"You're making a racket," Ginnie said hostilely. "Who were you talking to? Your mother *again*?"

George glanced back at the magazine and gulped, his addlepated mind flitting between delusion and reality. "No one," he said. "Just trying to get myself settled down. Can't sleep."

From the far side of the bathroom door, Ginnie expelled a deep, inhospitable sigh. "If you wake the girls, I'll murder you. Understand? Murder!"

"Okay, okay," George said defensively. "I'll keep it

down."

"You'd better!" Ginnie said. "Now good night."

When George returned to bed, he absently two-fingered the remaining pill on the bedstand, but finding it unneeded, slipped under the covers, pulled up them up, and fell instantly asleep. The rendezvous with his companion had brought about a sense of calm—distinct and clear, unlike any he'd known. Whether it was the dulcet sound of his companion's voice or those big brown eyes, he could not say. Only, that his presence had done something no pill ever could: provide a deep, near instant, slumber.

In the nights that followed, George took not a pill, but instead sought out his pal—who by some great miracle—always seemed available. They would talk by the hour, about any number of topics: marriage, child rearing, financial matters. George would seek out his advice, always to great effect. But above all, George was especially taken by his companion's spontaneity—of the sheer unexpectedness of his arrivals. For their encounters were soon no longer just of the late-night variety, but rather, and very often, in public of places: barbershops, restrooms, buffet lines, the commute home. Of late, they'd even played games: staring contests, Simon Says, charades were among their favorites. On nice days they liked to window-shop and on rainy ones, they would whisper sweet nothings from under an umbrella, and on especially romantic afternoons, when they felt especially bold, they would embrace on a street corner. To George's surprise, they agreed on everything: politics, religion, movies, music. Even sex. They had the same alma mater. Drove the same car. Laughed at the same jokes. In short, they were a perfect match.

On a Saturday, in the midst of a protracted, late-morning shave, George stood before the bathroom mirror with his companion staring back. "I really think you ought to switch over to a Braun electric," his companion was now just saying.

George Barbasoled up his face and frowned. "I don't get as close of a shave," he said pointedly. "As you know, I've a very heavy beard."

"The difference is negligible," his companion retorted. "Besides, I don't like seeing that pretty face of yours all cut up."

"Don't be silly," George said trying not to blush over his companion's concern. "With these new blades, it's a cinch."

The words were no sooner out of George's mouth when the razor he was holding skiffed across his neckline and cut into his flesh.

"See!" his companion said, unable to suppress a giggle. "That's what I was talking about. Now you've gone and made a mess of yourself."

George dropped the razor into the sink and reached for a hand towel. As blood streamed down the tricky slope of his neck, he managed to blot it out just before it reached the ribbed portion of undershirt. "Quit laughing," George said loudly and flicked a hand at his companion's cheek. "It isn't funny, you know. You can be very insensitive sometimes, you really should try to be more-"

From behind George came the barefooted steps of Ginnie. She held a blondish twin in the nook of her left arm and an even blonder one in her right. "George, who in God's name are you talking to?"

George looked at his wife and then back at the mirror, "No one."

"Every time I turn around lately you're talking to yourself," Ginnie said as she adjusted the twins in her arms. "You've got to stop. It isn't healthy."

"Bullshit! Leave us alone," came a strange, un-modulated baritone.

Ginnie staggered for a moment and very nearly dropped the twins. "How-how dare you!" she said. "How could you say such a thing?"

"*I* didn't say anything. It was him," George said nodding at the mirror. "My companion."

Ginnie set the twins down on the nearby changing table and sidled up to George. "What's going on, George? What in God's name is happening?"

George looked not at his wife, or his own reflection, but rather, at the person in the mirror.

"There's someone I want you to meet," George said after a moment.

Ginnie looked at the mirror and then back to George again.

"Have you lost your mind?" she said as she shook her head incomprehensibly. "Are you kidding me?"

George waited for his companion to speak on his behalf, but seeing he wasn't quite up to it, decided to just come out with it:

"I haven't had to take a pill since we met," George confessed, again nodding at the mirror. "Every night we talk and then I'm able to sleep like a baby. We've become good, good friends."

With her mouth agape, Ginnie slowly began to tear up. She then grabbed George by his shoulders and began to shake him vigorously. "I'm calling Dr. Seabring!" she said. "This funny business with the mirror has got stop, George.

Understand? It's got to stop!"

"Seabring's a hack," George scoffed. "Besides, I haven't gone to a session in weeks. He's useless."

Ginnie stood for a moment very nearly teetering over. And then she was off, racing about the house floor to floor, breaking every mirror in sight. When she was done, she walked indiscriminately through the shards of mirror that lay about the floor and picked up the phone. "I'm calling your mother! Understand, George? Your mother!"

It took George most of the night to convince Ginnie that he'd be fine alone for a few hours. That when she picked up Mother at the train station it would be better if he weren't there. They could talk. Strategize. Arrive at some decisive conclusion. By morning she'd gone along with it, even agreed to take the twins along.

"Now you're sure you'll be alright by yourself?" Ginnie asked sticking her head out the open car window.

George tapped the window at the twins in the back seat and smiled. "I'll be fine," he said looking Ginnie squarely in the eye. "Now that I've got a few doses of pills in my system, I'm already starting to feel better."

Ginnie gave George a hard look as though seeking some sign, some indication that her husband was in trouble. "Well, you certainly are acting more like yourself," she said. "But listen, just take it easy, will ya? And don't try any of that mirror business."

George put his left hand in the pocket of his corduroys and squeezed at the shard of mirror he'd been hiding since last night. "I won't," he said assuredly. "Like I said, I'm already feeling better."

"Alright then," Ginnie said and shifted the car into

reverse. "I'd better get going."

George nodded and blew the twins a kiss, all the while thinking of the unbridgeable gap between them.

George entered the house and pulled out four sealed envelopes. Inscribed in his signature block lettering were the following designations: WIFE, DAUGHTER, DAUGHTER, MOTHER. He'd been unable to bring himself to write their actual names. For despite what he would soon do, they were the women in his life, and though he rarely used the term, he loved them, in all their assorted goodness. As a means of softening the blow, he'd contemplated addressing them with a term of endearment—with a strong preference for Dollface or Babycakes—but at the urging of his companion, opted for the more conventional descriptors. After taking a moment to admire his penmanship, George moved from bedroom to bedroom and placed an envelope on the corresponding pillowcase. While there were some minor variations between them, each missive conveyed the same underlying sentiment: he was going away. With his companion. Indefinitely. That there'd be no point in tracking him down—he'd be otherwise occupied and, for all intents and purposes, unreachable.

From a distant room, George's companion was calling. His voice had a deeper register than his own and more than vaguely resembled that of his late father.

"We've still got to hammer out the final details," his companion said. "The logistics."

There was concern in his companion's baritone, George noted. "Don't worry. I'll be right there," he replied. "Lickety-split."

George lingered in the solitude of the twin's' bedroom, and at that key, unobjectionable moment, there was no place he'd rather be. He remembered painting it; he thought of he and Ginnie endlessly pouring over color swatches, of finally settling on something called "'butternut.'" As he studied the walls and the fine work of yellow he'd done, a minor, latent bit of pride came into his mental aspect: this was a happy room he thought. The whole house was, as a matter of fact. As he closed his eyes, he imagined what it would be like when they found him—a room, a house, forever tainted by a singular, horrific act. Bridging his hand across his nose, George suddenly felt a trifle unbalanced and plunked down in a rocking chair. The room smelled of unopened diapers and baby lotion. They were things Ginnie bought, things entirely apart from him; a stockpile of items he thought—each one filling up the rather outsized warehouse that was his detachment.

Just then, George became aware of cigarette smoke wafting his way. He wasn't a smoker himself, but his companion was, and regrettably, he knew the odor all too well. Still, as he joined his companion in the guest bedroom, he couldn't resist watching in amazement as smoke ring after smoke ring cascaded to the ceiling. He'd attempted the trick himself on a few occasions, but always failed—never quite sure what part of his technique was faulty.

"What took you so long?" his companion asked.

George propped up the shard of mirror that had been in his pocket on the chiffonier and shook his head. "I was only but a minute," he said rather defensively. "You know perfectly well I had to deal with the envelopes."

"I don't know why you'd bother," his companion said

offhandedly and blew another smoke ring toward the ceiling. "It's only going to make things harder."

George let out a sigh. The only other sound in the house was the purr of the basement furnace. "That's easy for you to say," he said. "*I'm* the one that has to do all the dirty work."

"Now don't go and start up with *that* again," his companion said. "After all, we *both* agreed to this thing. We *both* have a part to play."

George's eyes played around the room and then, all at once, he looked between, through, and past the immediate face of his companion, "I'm sorry"," he said. "I'm just nervous is all."

"I can tell," his companion said as he placed a reassuring hand on his shoulder. "Everything's going to be okay, though, George. *I* promise."

George averted his gaze from his companion's eyes as his own began to tear up. "I hate for you to see me like this," he said as he wiped at his eyes. "I'm just really, really struggling."

"Now, don't look so glum," his companion said. "This is *supposed* to be a happy occasion. Besides, I've a present for you."

George stared at his companion and blinked. "A present?" He then watched as his companion silently handed over an object from the waistband of his pants.

"This belonged to my father," George said as he turned the object over in his hands.

His companion smiled back. "It's a Walther 7.65. I found it among your father's effects," his companion explained. "The box was labeled 'wartime relics.'"

George nodded in agreement, but remained transfixed

by the object in his hands. "He was a collector," George said. "Used to have a roomful of German items: lighters, binoculars, canteens—that sort of thing."

"You're pleased then?" his companion asked. "This makes you happy?"

George inched closer to the shard of mirror propped up on the bookshelf till he and his companion's nose were very nearly touching. "Very," he said, as his breath fogged up the mirror ever so slightly. "Very."

"Good," his companion said. "Good. Now how about the door?"

George set the Walther on the bureau and, following his companion's gaze, looked at the locked door of the guest bathroom. He then reached a hand into his left front pocket and with a soupçon of fanfare, pulled out a key, and inserted it into the keyhole till there was a click.

"There," George said, and with a smile on his face he looked back at his companion.

"Bravo, my friend. Bravo!" his companion said and clapped his hands together. "A spare key? Where in God's name did you get that?"

George straightened to an upright position and eyed the mirror. "I grew up in this house," he replied, looking pleased with himself. "*I* know where everything is. Everything!"

The ringing of the phone jarred George from a long ponderous silence, the kind he'd grown so prone to at unguarded moments.

George backed away from the shard of mirror and picked up the line. "Hello?"

"George?" Ginnie said rhetorically. "Listen, your

mother's train is delayed. Might be a couple hours."

George adjusted the angle of the phone and looked over at the shard of mirror balanced on an opposite bookshelf. He then gave his companion a quick look. "That's okay," he replied nonchalantly into the phone.

"Are you sure?" Ginnie asked. "Want me to send someone over? I think Mrs. Clobridge is around."

George paused as his companion gesticulated wildly in the background. "No," George said, doing his best to keep an even voice. "We'll-I mean, I'll-, *I'll* be fine."

"Are you sure you're alright? You sound funny," Ginnie said. "You haven't been doing any of the mirror business, have you?"

George expelled a laugh. "Of course not," he said. "I told you, I'm done with that stuff. Besides, how could I? The only mirror left in the house is in the guestroom, and as you well know, you've gone and locked it on me."

There was a brief pause in the conversation as one and then both of the twins began crying in the background. "Hold on a sec," Ginnie said.

As George listened to the twins cry, a trembling melody of fear overcame him to the point that he very nearly dropped the phone.

"Listen, George," Ginnie said a moment later, "I gotta go. "Zinna needs a diaper change. But look, promise me you'll behave yourself."

George cleared his throat as he battled to keep himself together. "Of course," he said cheerfully. "Of course."

"Alright then," Ginnie said as though she were suddenly in a hurry. "Should be home in a few hours. Five. Fivish. Okay?"

"Okay," George said, "Goodbye."

"Promise me you'll be good, George," Ginnie demanded. "Promise me."

"I promise," George said and tears billowed down his face. "I promise, now goodbye," and the line went dead.

With time to spare, George's companion suggested they eat something. After all, where they'd be going would be no place for an empty stomach. In fact, why not go all out? Order from that little place down the street. Maybe even get something sweet.

The feast arrived in no less than thirty minutes: egg rolls, spring rolls, crab Rangoon, egg drop soup, bang bang ji, Dou ban yu, Kung Pao chicken, Moo Shu pork. They took turns feeding each other over the din of Gershwin, intermittently pausing to dab each other's mouth. For dessert, they shared a half moon cookie. Their favorite. As they devoured the last of it, the clarion tones of "Let's Call the Whole Thing Off" played:

> *Things have come to a pretty pass*
> *Our romance is growing flat,*
> *For you like this and the other*
> *While I go for this and that,*
> *Goodness knows what the end will be*
> *Oh I don't know where I'm at*
> *It looks as if we two will never be one*
> *Something must be done.*

George began to keep time by slapping his hands together and stomping his feet. He egged his companion to join in, but to no avail. As the second verse began, he sensed a surge of disenchantment on the part of his dearie, but being so caught up in song, ignored him.

But oh, if we call the whole thing off then we must part
And oh, if we ever part, then that might break my hea-

Without warning, George's companion reached over and snapped off the arm of his father's Columbia Grafonola phonograph, and the living room was startlingly quiet. It was an uncomfortable silence, the kind generally reserved for couples and that was customarily followed by some great, often horrific, domestic wrangle. What ensued was a series of wild muscle twitches and near convulsions that a passing observer would construe as nothing more than a man peacefully staring off into the distance, for the reverberations were internal, if not altogether imagined. Minutes later, George cast a look askance toward his companion's and exited the house.

Outside, George recalled sanity with grave sentimental reverence. Not unlike a grown man passing by his boyhood home. The tree house. The sandbox. The swing set. The apple grove. They stood like signposts to the now vacant ramshackle home: his mind. As he made his final inspection of the house proper, he remembered overcoming the sleeping problem. How he no longer needed all those pills. Telling Dr. Seabring to fuck off. That he'd be fine. And now, here he was, fine—merely wanting to disappear with his dearest and only friend.

Minutes later, George tiptoed inside the house and up the stairs before his companion could take notice. From under a mattress, he pulled out his copy of *Time* magazine, looked at it briefly, and then continued across the room, cradling the object. Standing hipshot, he dropped the item into the sink. He studied it a moment, as though calculating, measuring the consequences. For although it was a petty act, the object he was about to set aflame would set things right—would make *them* even. George proceeded to take a deep breath, exhaled, and then, from his pocket, he pulled out a German infantry issued lighter, circa 1944. As flame engulfed the upper left corner of the magazine, it began to curl. Soon, there was nothing in the sink but ash— that and a small, nearly microscopic piece of the reflective cover, which he pocketed. Then abruptly and familiarly, George dressed himself in his father's best Brooks Brother's suit.

Presently, each stood before the other, staring deeply, methodically into the other's eyes. For a full half hour they debated, proposed, counter-proposed, refuted, rebutted, screamed, and even slapped. But now they had made their decision. Now they knew what must be done. And both were completely and utterly comfortable with it. In retrospect, they both agreed they had been silly, and wondered how such a thing could have taken so long to decide. After all, it was the obvious, *sensible* thing to do. And now, at last, when everything was agreed upon, George suddenly noticed his head was throbbing. He opened the mirrored cabinet, grabbed the aspirin, and dry swallowed two pills. Before he could close the cabinet though, he heard tires screech: Ginnie? He checked his watch: 4:30. By now mother would be off the train. But likely in the middle of rush hour traffic. Still, he hustled to the window: the neighbor's dog had gotten lose, its shirtless owner in the midst of chasing it down. With the ruckus seemingly over, George continued to stare out: the lawn was overdue, the driveway should be resealed, the garage door needed a paint job. As George stared back at his collective neglect, he felt, if only for a second, a tinge of guilt. And then, just as quickly, he was summoned:

"George? Are you ready?"

George looked out the window one more time and then turned back to face his companion. "Yes," he replied, "I'm ready."

"Good. Very good," his companion said and smiled. "Now let me have a look at you."

At the sink, George closed the mirror, noting his companion held something at his side. He recognized it as the "'present'" he'd received earlier in the day, only now it was somehow different—perhaps best characterized as "loaded."

He hadn't had ahold of the thing since the day he'd snatched it from his father's belongings. He'd taken it as a last-minute souvenir, a keepsake really. That had been a mouth-set-tight day. One of those long, protracted days of unbelonging. Everyone had spoken in half-tones or simply not at all. Such was the house. They, as in the foursome that was the Martians, had been in need of God-help. He'd looked everywhere, but there was no crying-partner, no late-model children to save him. Instead he felt emptyish, and there was no one to share the darkness, just an afterthing, a face looking back at him that was God-statured, soul-struck, unbodied. Now came the great reckoning of an unlaureled life. To, at long last, be heart-won!

George paced back and forth any number of times, expelling pockets of hot, nervous breath. Finally, he mustered the resolve and cocked the piece.

"Keep your nerve!" his companion shouted. "Keep your

nerve, Goddamn you!"

Somewhere in distance, over the resonant pulsebeats of his heart, George heard a car pull in. Seconds later, the front door slammed. Then came the crying of the twins. The crying.

"Pull the trigger, Goddamn you!" his companion commanded. "Otherwise this'll be one Christly mess!"

George raised the Walther PPK 7.65 to shoulder height and pulled the trigger: the bullet discharged from the chamber with breathtaking ease and, with even less effort, found the right temple of its victim. Whether it struck George Patrick Martian, age 36, of 424 Weaver Street, or that of his reflection, was impossible to say.

ABOUT ATMOSPHERE PRESS

Atmosphere Press is an independent full-service publisher for books in genres ranging from nonfiction to fiction to poetry, with a special emphasis on being an author-friendly approach to the challenges of getting a book into the world. Learn more about what we do at atmospherepress.com.

We encourage you to check out some of Atmosphere's latest releases, which are available at Amazon.com and via order from your local bookstore:

No Home Like a Raft, poetry by Martin Jon Porter

Mere Being, poetry by Barry D. Amis

The Traveler, a young adult novel by Jennifer Deaver

Mandated Happiness, a novel by Clayton Tucker

The Third Door, a novel by Jim Williams

The Yoga of Strength, a novel by Andrew Marc Rowe

To the Next Step: Your Guide from High School and College to The Real World, nonfiction by Kyle Grappone

They are Almost Invisible, poetry by Elizabeth Carmer

Let the Little Birds Sing, a novel by Sandra Fox Murphy

Carpenters and Catapults: A Girls Can Do Anything Book, children's fiction by Carmen Petro

Spots Before Stripes, a novel by Jonathan Kumar

Auroras over Acadia, poetry by Paul Liebow

Channel: How to be a Clear Channel for Inspiration by Listening, Enjoying, and Trusting Your Intuition, nonfiction by Jessica Ang

Gone Fishing: A Girls Can Do Anything Book, children's fiction by Carmen Petro

Owlfred the Owl, a picture book by Caleb Foster

Love Your Vibe: Using the Power of Sound to Take Command of Your Life, nonfiction by Matt Omo

Transcendence, poetry and images by Vincent Bahar Towliat

Leaving the Ladder: An Ex-Corporate Girl's Guide from the Rat Race to Fulfilment, nonfiction by Lynda Bayada

Adrift, poems by Kristy Peloquin

Letting Nicki Go: A Mother's Journey through Her Daughter's Cancer, nonfiction by Bunny Leach

Time Do Not Stop, poems by William Guest

Dear Old Dogs, a novella by Gwen Head

Bello the Cello, a picture book by Dennis Mathew

How Not to Sell: A Sales Survival Guide, nonfiction by Rashad Daoudi

Ghost Sentence, poems by Mary Flanagan

That Scarlett Bacon, a picture book by Mark Johnson

Such a Nice Girl, a novel by Carol St. John

Makani and the Tiki Mikis, a picture book by Kosta Gregory

What Outlives Us, poems by Larry Levy

Winter Park, a novel by Graham Guest

That Beautiful Season, a novel by Sandra Fox Murphy

What I Cannot Abandon, poems by William Guest

All the Dead Are Holy, poems by Larry Levy

Rescripting the Workplace: Producing Miracles with Bosses, Coworkers, and Bad Days, nonfiction by Pam Boyd

Surviving Mother, a novella by Gwen Head

Who Are We: Man and Cosmology, poetry by William Guest

ABOUT THE AUTHOR

Christopher Gould is a graduate of Nazareth College of Rochester where he earned a degree in Writing. His fiction and poetry have appeared in several literary magazines and anthologies. Gould is a teacher in upstate New York where he lives with his wife and daughter.

The George Stories is his first novel.